I always get what I want . . . That's Dr Richard West's proud boast, and looking at all the expensive equipment he's acquired for the Intensive Care Unit at County General, Sister Charmian Williams can well believe it. Surely such a brilliant, good-looking and persuasive man can be refused nothing? So when he turns his attentions to Charmian what hope does she have of resistance . . .

INTENSIVE AFFAIR

BY
ANN JENNINGS

MILLS & BOON LIMITED
London · Sydney · Toronto

First published in Great Britain 1984
by Mills & Boon Limited, 15–16 Brook's Mews,
London W1A 1DR

Australian copyright 1984
Philippine copyright 1984

ISBN 0 263 74759 X

Set in 10 on 11½ pt Linotron Times
03–0784–55,500

Photoset by Rowland Phototypesetting Ltd
Bury St Edmunds, Suffolk
Made and printed in Great Britain by
Richard Clay (The Chaucer Press) Ltd
Bungay, Suffolk

CHAPTER ONE

THE FAMILIAR antiseptic smell of the hospital which, mixed with the smell of cooking from the canteen, drifted in through an open window, did little to reassure Charmian. She walked slowly down the hospital corridor, delaying the moment when she knew she had to sit in the waiting-room before the interview. She was feeling very nervous and wondered whether she had made herself look old enough for the sister's job she was applying for. Although she was twenty-five she was always being accused of looking seventeen, so today she had pulled her silvery hair into a severe knot on the top of her head and secured it firmly with a wooden pin. Her hair was naturally very fair but she had dark, arched brows and a delicate olive-coloured skin which made the startling ultramarine of her eyes, fringed with thick dark lashes, the first thing most people noticed. This morning, like every other morning, she wore no make-up except for a translucent pale pink lipstick, which subtly accentuated the sensuous curve of her wide mouth.

In spite of her enforced leisurely pace she was unable to delay the moment of arrival any longer and at last she was there. Taking a deep breath, so as not to appear nervous, she knocked on the door of the appointed room and walked swiftly in. Her quick gaze took in the occupants and she saw that there were three other women waiting. She noticed with slight dismay that they all seemed to be at least ten years older than herself!

After giving her name to the secretary at the desk she

joined the other three, who were all in uniform. She suddenly wondered if she should have worn her own uniform instead of the dress she had chosen, but her worry was short-lived, for she had only time to cross her slim legs when the door to the adjoining room opened.

'Miss Williams! Please come in now.'

Startled, Charmian stood up. She hadn't realised that the interviews would start so soon. Hastily she smoothed her skirt and brushed an imaginary hair into place. She felt flustered and nervous but she gave no outward sign of it as she walked with lissom grace into the room.

Within, there were four people sitting behind two large desks, and placed strategically in front of them was a single chair. A pleasant nondescript looking young man was sitting at one of the desks and he got up as Charmian entered the room.

'Miss Williams?' he said with a slight inflexion in his voice.

Charmian nodded and was about to reply when another voice cut sarcastically across, a deep voice with a faint Scots twang to it.

'I hope the whole interview won't be conducted in mime.'

Charmian drew in her breath with a sharp anger. 'I've hardly had time to open my mouth yet,' she retorted, 'but I can assure you that I am quite capable of speech.' She turned her head as she spoke and looked into a pair of dark brown, unfathomable eyes.

Never taking his eyes off her he lazily unfurled his tall frame and stood up extending his hand in greeting. 'I'm Dr West, Richard West, consultant in charge of Intensive Care,' he said evenly. 'So you see, I am very interested in your reactions.'

He was tall, taller than most men—Charmian realised as

he towered over her, and was dark with a lean, intelligent face. He surveyed her with just the faintest hint of mockery. She felt the blood rushing to her cheeks and her heart thumped in her breast so loudly she thought the whole room must hear it. Trembling slightly as she politely put her slim hand in his, she was surprised that he clasped it so firmly and felt annoyed that her pulse was racing uncontrollably, much faster than she had ever known before. Coolly, she removed her hand and looked back defiantly into his dark veiled eyes.

'How do you do,' she said and, taking a step backwards, sat down carefully in the chair being proffered by the young man who had first spoken to her.

'May I take your coat?' he asked. 'It is rather stuffy in here.'

As she handed him her short cream jacket she wished she hadn't decided on the navy blue jersey dress but had stuck instead to her uniform At the time it had seemed businesslike but now, under the penetrating gaze of Richard West, she was only too well aware that it clung to the curves of her body and accentuated rather than disguised her shapely hips and long elegant thighs. Richard West's eyes slid in an appreciative gaze slowly and sensually down her body. Charmian felt her cheeks beginning to burn beneath his all-seeing gaze, and began to feel embarrassed and angry. How dare this man unnerve her like this! She caught his glance as his eyes came back to her face and held there defiantly.

'You are aware that we are looking for a senior sister for the Intensive Care Unit?' he asked in a derisive tone of voice.

The stress on the word senior made Charmian realise that even with her hair scraped up in such a severe style she didn't look very old. He was making it quite obvious that he didn't think she was old enough, or that she could possibly be experienced enough for the post.

'I am well aware of that fact,' she replied matching the tone of his voice with ice in her own and trying not to let the turbulent feelings within her show in her voice. 'I would not have applied for the post had I not felt sure that I was capable of doing the job.' In fact she spoke with a confidence she didn't possess, but by now her blood was up and any doubts she may have had were swept away by anger.

He made no answer but she was sure the defiant tone of her voice annoyed him from the way his eyes glinted and he leaned slowly forward to write something on the pad in front of him. She was very aware of his hand, huge, with long, strong sensitive fingers. It was with difficulty that she concentrated on the questions now being asked of her by the Senior Nursing Officer and the other woman who was the District Nursing Officer.

The young man at the desk, whose name was Clarke Thomas, asked her a lot of routine questions. He was the hospital's Personnel Officer and Charmian tried to concentrate on making all her answers businesslike and pleasant. At the end of the interview she stood up and shook hands with the two nursing officers first, then with Clarke Thomas, who clasped her hand warmly and smiled encouragingly at her. She turned stiffly to Richard West and against her will found her eyes hypnotically drawn to his. She had regained her composure by now, but as her fingers were gripped by his she felt unable to draw her eyes away from his face, and her breath caught suffocatingly in her throat. The warmth from his hand seemed to flow straight into her veins like fire, liquid tendrils reaching into her heart to make it pound uncontrollably. His eyes were amused and knowing, and a slight smile curved the edge of his hard mouth.

'If you will wait outside Miss Williams,' his voice seemed cold to her, 'we will let you know at the end of the interview who will be offered the post.'

Withdrawing her hand from his Charmian tipped her chin forward slightly, giving her a provocative air of confidence which in reality at that moment she didn't possess.

'Thank you,' she replied coolly. 'Good-morning, everyone.'

Clarke Thomas came across and handed her the cream jacket, which she folded over her arm with a natural grace. Then she walked silently out of the room.

Once outside she drew her breath in angrily. She had wanted this job so much, and now that wretched, arrogant, overbearing man had made her lose her cool. What was the matter with her? She was well-qualified, she was intelligent! And she was used to men looking at her with appraising eyes. Because of her striking good looks, plenty of men made passes at her and she had always handled them without difficulty. She had never met a man who could make her feel so . . . *so*, what was it? So vulnerable, yes that was it she thought restlessly. Vulnerable, unsure of herself, like a jittery schoolgirl. She wasn't used to feeling uncomfortable, she wasn't used to feeling out of control and she didn't like it. No, she decided quite emphatically, I do not like it at all!

She was suddenly aware that the other three women in the room were eyeing her curiously. Then the door opened and Clarke Thomas's voice called, 'Miss Smith.' The oldest looking of the three got up and went in.

Charmian looked at her. She looks a no-nonsense, sensible type she thought glumly, observing the regulation flat lace-up black shoes. I can't imagine her being thrown off balance by Richard West!

By the time everyone had been interviewed, Charmian had philosophically resigned herself to not getting the job. She was idly flicking through the *Nursing Mirror* when Clarke Thomas came out. He looked around the room and picked out Charmian.

'Miss Williams,' he said, 'would you come through?'

She could hardly believe her ears. Had she got the job? He ushered her back into the interview room and closed the door behind her, remaining outside himself with the other three candidates.

The Senior Nursing Officer stood up smiling. 'Miss Williams, my colleagues and I are pleased to offer you the post of sister to the Intensive Care Unit of this hospital.'

In a dream Charmian heard her own voice replying slowly, 'Thank you, I am pleased to accept the position.'

Richard West also stood up, and leaned slightly towards her across the table. 'Good,' he said briskly. 'Now what I want to know is, when can you start?'

Charmian was careful to avoid his eyes when replying. If I am going to work with this man I have got to learn to cope with his unnerving presence, she thought firmly. To her amazement she heard her voice answering without the suspicion of a tremor. 'My present contract finishes in ten days' time, at the end of the month.'

'Oh, I see,' he said sarcastically. 'You left it a little late in looking for a job!'

Charmian was about to flare back at him, but then, determined not to be ruffled by his insinuations, she ignored the remark and turned to the Senior Nursing Officer.

'I can extend my contract for another month, or start

at the beginning of next month, whichever is the most convenient to you.'

Richard West walked round the desk to her side. 'You will start in ten days' time,' he said quietly, in a voice that brooked no argument. 'And now, if Miss Smythe and Miss Woolner will excuse us, I will show you round the Intensive Care Unit before you leave.'

Miss Smythe and Miss Woolner nodded in mute agreement, and Charmian suddenly realised to her astonishment that they were frightened of him, absolutely terrified! Well, he's not going to frighten me she thought determinedly, and he's not going to catch me unaware again. I'm ready for him, she thought resolutely.

His dark eyes glimmered with some hidden emotion—she wasn't sure whether it was amusement or annoyance.

'You can come back and sign your contract later,' he said, and taking her arm propelled her out of the room.

Once outside Charmian wrenched her arm out of his grasp and then immediately regretted it. She felt foolish for over-reacting, but if he noticed he didn't show it. They carried on walking with long strides along the apparently never-ending corridor. All the time Dr West kept up a non-stop barrage of information about the Intensive Care Unit. When it opened, how many beds it had, how many nurses to each bed . . . Charmian couldn't help thinking how attractive the slight Scottish accent was as she tried to remember all the facts and figures he was flinging at her.

The hospital was a large one, very modern and built in a large square around a central well. This meant that all the rooms had daylight; the rooms on the outer perimeter of the square had views over the town and countryside to the sea. As the hospital was built on the top of a hill this meant that even the ground floor rooms had good views. The wards on the inside, overlooking the well, didn't have such a view but at least they had sunshine and everything was attractively laid out with ornamental bricks, a fountain, bushes and small trees.

Charmian had chosen this hospital, the County General, because it was away from London, but not too far away. Just over an hour by train, but distant enough, she thought, to feel as if it were in the middle of the country. Having spent all her childhood and, so far, all her working life in London, she longed to escape from the confines of the city like a bird longs to be free from a cage.

The hospital floors were identified by letters and as they went upstairs to D level where the ICU was situated, Charmian looked eagerly out of the windows. It was as they turned to go through the double doors to the Unit that she got her first glimpse of the sea,

'Oh!' she said involuntarily like a small girl, 'the sea!'

'Yes,' she heard an amused voice in her ear, '*the sea!*'

Charmian turned impulsively, her blue eyes shining. 'I've always wanted to be where I could see the sea.'

His stern mouth seemed almost gentle as he smiled at her enthusiasm. 'Well, not only will you be able to *see* the sea, you will smell it and I'm sure you will be taken sailing on it.'

He directed her through the double doors towards smaller doors on the other side of the corridor. There was a large sign marked Intensive Care on the wall and outside the double doors was a bell on the wall, and a notice asking visitors to ring and wait for someone to come.

He led her in. 'The changing room for you is there,' he said. 'Just put on overshoes, gown, cap and take a mask. You may need it.'

As she was slipping on the plastic overshoes, white gown which tied at the back, blue hat and mask, she began thinking of the questions she must ask him. She knew there was another sister working days on the Unit and wondered how their duties and responsibilities would be split.

It was almost as if he knew what she had been thinking, for he immediately said as she came through the door of the changing room, 'Now the first thing to do is to introduce you to the other sister. You will take alternate duties most of the time and cover each other for holidays. It will be left up to the two of you to sort your duties out.'

He introduced her with the minimum of formality to Sister Jefferies, who was a friendly, ginger-haired woman of about fifty years and it wasn't long before Charmian had met most of the unit staff.

Charmian was surprised to see the easy familiarity with which the other sister treated him. She called him Richard and he called her Liz. Suddenly he seemed different from when she had first met him, no longer so overbearing. He laughed and joked with Liz Jefferies and she seemed quite motherly towards him. Somehow I don't think *I* shall be able to feel motherly where he is concerned, thought Charmian wryly.

As they stood together talking, a junior doctor came up armed with sheafs of pathology reports and trailing an ECG monitor printout behind him. Richard West immediately gave him all his attention, looking at the ECG record and the pathology reports.

'How is his ECG and blood pressure now?' she heard

him ask. 'And have you sent off fresh samples to pathology?'

The registrar, whose name was John Bourne, had been pointed out to her by Liz Jefferies, along with other nurses and technicians who were all busily going about their business with the patients. Each patient was separated from his or her neighbour by a glass partition, but all the patients could be seen at a glance from the duty desk.

Richard West came back to Liz and Charmian. 'Come and see my latest equipment,' he said. 'This patient is as yet undiagnosed and has many puzzling symptoms. This,' indicating an enormous mass of electronic monitoring equipment, 'is monitoring everything so we can see how quickly he responds to various types of medication. Hopefully a clear pattern will emerge soon and we shall be able to come to some firm conclusions.'

Charmian pulled on her mask and followed him over to the bay where the patient was. She looked at the impressive range of equipment and at the poor man attached to it all.

'I can see why this unit is nicknamed "Expensive Scare",' she said, raising her eyebrows.

He turned quickly, a question in his voice. 'You don't approve?'

'Of course I approve,' Charmian replied quickly, 'so long as you don't make the mistake of thinking electronic equipment can take the place of good nursing and medical practice.'

She could see Liz Jefferies, out of the corner of her eye, nodding her head in vigorous approval of her statement.

'It will never take its place, but it is a very helpful addition,' he said. 'Take this non-invasive blood pressure monitoring system. It's so much more comfortable for the patient.'

He drew her over to look at what was obviously his latest acquisition for the unit. 'A blood pressure monitor that by means of a comfortable, painless cuff on the patient's arm, gives a continuous accurate monitoring of systolic, diastolic and mean arterial blood pressures, as well as heart rate.' He leaned back looking at it with a gleam of satisfaction in his eyes.

Charmian had never seen such a sophisticated piece of equipment. 'It must have been very expensive,' she said.

'Oh,' laughed Liz joining them, 'he is very good at persuading charities to donate him the equipment he wants.'

'I believe in going after what I want and not stopping until I get it.' His dark eyes looking over the top of his mask glinted mockingly at her. Charmian was glad of the mask she wore and hoped it was hiding most of the blush that stained her cheeks. She had an uneasy feeling he wasn't just referring to hospital equipment. She stared back at him stonily, trying to retrieve her previous composure.

Abruptly he turned and started walking away. 'I'll leave you with Liz for fifteen minutes or so,' he said over his shoulder, 'while I go and see a patient in theatre recovery who is due to be transferred here.'

Charmian turned her attention to Liz, who showed her where her office was. 'I'm afraid you'll have to share it with me,' she said apologetically, 'but I'm fairly tidy, and I think there should be plenty of room for both of us.'

Over a cup of coffee in their shared office Liz explained that the ICU had recently been expanded from six to ten beds and that Richard West had decided it needed two sisters to work alternate duties. As usual, and against all odds, he had got what he wanted. Charmian wondered whether Liz had minded someone else being appointed sister as well as her, but as she overtly studied her she could see that she really was a genuinely nice person and seemed to be easy going in a very sensible way. It was obvious that all the staff respected her and Charmian knew she would have to work hard to earn the same respect for herself.

'Don't let Richard upset you,' Liz said suddenly. 'I've known him since he was a houseman, and he can be . . . well, he can be a little difficult sometimes.'

Charmian raised her eyebrows. 'I *had* noticed,' she replied evenly. 'It won't bother me in the slightest—our relationship will be a strictly working one. Outside of my time on the unit I shall never give him a thought.' Even as she spoke she knew in the back of her mind that half of her was hoping that it would not be strictly work. The other half of her was telling her not to be so stupid and that he was probably married with half a dozen children. And he was obviously an absolutely impossible man anyway!

Liz was very friendly and helpful and assisted Charmian in getting everything sorted out so that she could start work in ten days' time. She had even planned a rough schedule of work, dividing the time between them evenly.

'If you have anything special on and would like time off, don't hesitate to ask,' she said. 'I'm single and I don't go out much. Just me, my cat and garden. So I'm not over-fussed about when I work.'

'Me neither,' Charmian assured her. 'I have nothing in particular to do in my spare time.'

'A pretty girl like you should have,' Liz retorted smartly.

Charmian wondered whether to confide in her or not for a moment, then, deciding she might as well said, 'My fiancé was killed in a car accident just over a year ago and it's just that . . . Well, I've never met anyone else,' she tailed off lamely.

Liz turned and squeezed her hand in a motherly fashion, and Charmian was glad she had confided in her. 'I've just a few words of advice to you, young lady,' she said briskly. 'Don't waste your life grieving for the dead. You must get on with the business of living, and that includes having men friends.'

Charmian was about to ask her what went wrong in *her* life, then thought better of it. 'Yes,' she just said meekly.

Richard West hadn't come back to the Unit by the time they had finished talking so Liz suggested that Charmian should go with her to the hospital canteen for lunch. As they walked down the miles of hospital corridors Charmian reflected that this hospital seemed much larger than the one she was used to in London. 'I know this hospital has more beds than the one I'm used to,' she remarked to Liz, 'but even so, the corridors seem extraordinarily long.'

Liz laughed. 'They do!' she agreed. 'It's because of the design of the wretched place. The huge square means we all have to walk miles. I reckon we nurses ought to get a pay rise just to pay for the extra pairs of shoes we wear out!'

The canteen was an enormous sunny room, pleasantly decorated with luxuriant pot plants. The atmosphere was rather like that of a commercial restaurant, it had managed to completely avoid the clinical influence of the hospital.

Liz and Charmian queued up, collected their lunch

from the self-service counter and sat at an empty table. 'I hope the Unit is quiet when I first start,' Charmian remarked, munching through her rather tough piece of chicken. 'It's my first job as sister, you know.' Somehow she didn't mind confiding her doubts to Liz.

'I shouldn't count on it being quiet,' said a masculine voice in her ear. Startled Charmian turned to find Richard West seating himself next to her. 'And that piece of chicken looks as if it could do with intensive therapy,' he said leaning over and looking at the shrivelled piece of meat with distaste.

Charmian couldn't help laughing. 'Yes, I can see now why most people stick to omelette and chips.' Both Richard West and Liz had chosen omelette and chips.

A large elderly man came and joined them. Richard introduced him as Dr Edwards, Consultant Cardiologist. Dr Edwards eyed Charmian's trim figure appreciatively. 'If you ever get tired of intensive care, you can come and be sister in cardiac catheters,' he said.

'And what about Sister Smith?' interrupted Liz.

Dr Edwards looked uncomfortable and shuffled in his seat. 'I mean of course when Sister Smith has retired,' he said hastily.

'Sister Williams will be married and retired herself by then,' said Liz, 'won't you Charmian?'

'Well, I . . . er,' murmured Charmian at a loss for something to say.

'Will you?' said Richard loudly, fixing Charmian with a piercing gaze, 'Do you have a fiancé then?'

'No I don't,' replied Charmian rising and picking up her tray, feeling that if she wasn't careful the conversation would rapidly get out of control.

'Do you have a regular male friend?' persisted Richard rudely.

'It's really none of your business,' said Charmian tartly, his keen glance unnerving her.

'It is just that I like my sisters to keep their minds on their job,' he said curtly, 'and not to have emotional entanglements clogging their wits.'

'I can assure you that my personal life will not "clog my wits" as you so eloquently put it,' Charmian flared back at him. 'Now if you will excuse us . . .' Nodding briefly at a rather startled Dr Edwards she left the table, Liz following her.

Liz had arranged for a small hospital flat to be available for her and after they had finished in the canteen and Charmian had been to the personnel office to sign her contract, which had been left ready for her by Clarke Thomas with a little hand written note apologising for his absence and hoping to see her again when she started, she set off to find her flat.

Slowly she walked down the long tree-lined avenue which sloped gently down the hill away from the hospital. She took in great breaths of fresh air. It was a gorgeously sunny day and the air was crisp and intoxicatingly fresh. She eventually found the house where her flat was situated without difficulty. It was a one-bedroomed flat with kitchen-cum-dining room, a large lounge and an adequate bathroom. All completely self-contained and private. The flat itself was part of a very large Victorian house, set in an enormous, rambling, attractively overgrown garden. As it was springtime the garden was a kaleidoscope of yellow, blue, green and purple. There were huge drifts of daffodils and bluebells, the hedge was of forsythia which was in full bloom, a blaze of brilliant yellow. She could see lilac bushes at the far end of the garden—they were enormous and covered with full, fat buds.

The house itself was built of warm red brick and its old walls were covered in climbing roses, not in bloom at this time of year, not even in leaf, but the branches were covered in red tipped shoots, the promise of masses of flowers to come, and they gave the sides of the house a misty, rosy hue. Charmian felt a surge of happiness. She felt she was really in the country! From her kitchen and lounge windows she looked down into the garden at the back of the house, where there was a large rather unkempt lawn, surrounded by spring flowers. The flat was furnished in a simple manner with cane funiture and all the walls were cream, which suited Charmian fine. She had few belongings but in her mind's eye she could see that they would fit in well.

My Indian tapestry will go on that wall there, she thought, and I can put my bookcase there. My *cloisonné* vase will look perfect in that alcove. A million ideas raced through her head.

The residence manager had kindly given her the key and told her that she could move in any time she wanted during the next ten days. Charmian planned to come down from London, lock, stock and barrel at the weekend when she was off duty, and move in then. Then she wouldn't be in a last minute rush before commencing work at the County General. She also had four days leave to take, so that would neatly finish off her contract and give her the weekend plus four days, Monday to Thursday, to move in and get to know the town that was soon to become her new home. According to the rota Liz had drawn up she would then start work on the Friday and also be on duty her first weekend.

As she wandered around the flat her attention was suddenly drawn to a large cupboard over the doorway into the lounge. It appeared to be set in the wall. Curious to find out what it contained, she got a stool from the kitchen and clambered on top of it to try to open the doors. They appeared to be stuck fast. Charmian struggled with the knob, twisting this way and that, until suddenly it sprang open with such force that she lost her balance. As she started to fall she grabbed at the door frame in an effort to save herself—but instead of crashing to the floor a pair of strong arms enveloped her, holding her as lightly as if she were a feather, and saved her from falling.

Charmian was aware of iron strong muscles rippling beneath the Aran sweater, and that Richard West was in that sweater. He made no effort to let her go but looked down at her with a quizzical gaze.

'It's just as well I looked in to see if you liked your flat,' he said in a low voice. 'Otherwise you might have started off in the County General as a patient, not a nurse!'

For a wild, almost ecstatic moment, Charmian thought he was going to kiss her. His dark head was bent close to hers and she could feel the warmth of his breath on her cheek and smell the faint, masculine odour of his aftershave. He had an open-necked shirt on under his sweater and she was very conscious of the mass of dark curling hair at the base of his throat. She felt herself succumbing weakly to the sheer masculinity of the man, and put up her hands in a protective gesture pushing him away. He tightened his arms slightly at the pressure of her hands, then suddenly relaxed and, letting her go, pushed her a little distance from him. But still he kept his hands firmly anchored round her slim waist.

'You are too thin,' he said. 'I can almost get my hands around your waist.' As he spoke he tightened them.

Charmian struggled to keep a clear head and, putting her hands on his, prized them away.

'Thank you for catching me,' she murmured.

She was feeling badly shaken. She had been totally unprepared for the way she had responded to the contact of his body. His innate virility brought turbulent, long-subdued feelings of total femininity reeling to the surface and Charmian instinctively felt she must put a distance between them. His dark brooding eyes seemed to mock her as he responded to the pressure of her slender fingers and let her go, but he said nothing, just smiled briefly and strolled over to the window.

Charmian stayed where she was and the short distance that separated them enabled her to look at him properly for the first time. The sunlight through the window illuminated his strong profile with its well-defined nose, sculptured lips and chin. He had a mass of dark hair, well cut but looking as if it would curl if left to its own devices. She wondered if he was a keen sailor as he was tanned on the face and throat. His whole appearance was totally masculine, devastatingly, attractively masculine. She felt herself reacting to his masculinity even now, when they were separated physically by some yards.

He turned towards her and Charmian realised too late that her hair had fallen out of its restraining pin and was cascading down onto her shoulders. Self-consciously she put up a hand to twist it up again.

'Don't,' he said, stepping over and pulling her hand down. With his other hand he picked up a handful of her silvery hair and let it run through his fingers. Charmian felt like the proverbial rabbit hypnotised by a snake, unable to move, to speak, to breathe hardly. His dark, smouldering eyes held hers, his body moved closer and she could feel the strength of his muscled thighs against her slim body. His hand left her hair and softly rested on her shoulders, imperceptibly pressing her body closer to his. It seemed in her taut imagination that they were fusing into one being, they were so close.

Although the whole episode took only a fleeting second, it seemed to Charmian like a lifetime before she gathered up her reserves of will-power and pushed him away. She kept her eyes averted from his. She didn't want this man to see the depths of passion he had disturbed. Trying not to let her voice tremble she said, 'I think you had better leave now Dr West, as I have things to do. I must take some measurements so that I can plan where to put my things . . .' Her voice trailed off awkwardly into silence.

For a moment she thought he was going to refuse, for he stood perfectly still, saying nothing, just looking at her with his dark brooding eyes. Then, moving quickly away, he stepped past her and out of the door.

'Yes,' he said huskily, 'I think perhaps you are right. I mustn't interrupt you for any longer.' Then as suddenly as he had arrived, he was gone.

Charmian shut the door slowly behind him and leaned against it breathing unevenly. She felt angry with herself for responding so readily to his sexual attraction and angry with him for presuming that an acquaintance of a few hours gave him the right to take her in his arms. Or *had* he taken her in his arms? Was she reading more into it than there actually was? In her confused state she couldn't be absolutely certain.

Perhaps he thought I was encouraging him when he caught me, she thought. Admittedly she didn't resist very actively! As she prepared to leave for the station to catch the train back to London, Charmian made a resolution that she was not, definitely not, going to get involved with this man. He was her boss and that was how he was going to stay, nothing more. It was going to be a strictly professional relationship.

The more she thought about it the more annoyed she became with herself and also with him, although common sense told her that he was probably completely unaware of the effect he had on her. The conflicting thoughts churned over and over in her mind so that by the time she reached London she was almost ready to hand in her notice for a job she had not even started!

She was still undecided about what to do until she opened the door of her poky London room, the windows of which looked out onto the dirty bricks of the tower block next door. Then, remembering the lovely old house with her flat in it and the garden full of spring flowers, she slammed the door shut in a positive manner behind her.

Hell, she thought rebelliously, why should I let a mere man spoil things for me? He most likely thinks that because he's good-looking he can have any woman he wants! That accounts for his arrogant air. He said he always got what he wanted! Well, just for once he is going to be disappointed. He has met a woman who is not going to succumb to his charms. She took a deep, determined breath. Most definitely not!

CHAPTER TWO

IN THE next few days that followed, Charmian was so busy organising her move that the memory of Richard West's disturbing presence began to fade slowly into the back of her mind.

Finally the last day at her old hospital arrived. The nurses from the mens' surgical ward she was leaving had thrown a party for her on the final Friday night. It was the usual hospital party, everyone crammed into a small room off the side of the ward, so that the people on duty wouldn't miss out on all the fun, and assorted bottles of wine assembled, to be drunk out of glasses scrounged from patients' bedside lockers! Sister Evans, who was usually a bit of a dragon, had come and after three glasses of wine was distinctly merry. She proceeded to horrify the two new housemen with tales of what she used to get up to when she was younger!

Charmian thoroughly enjoyed herself. It seemed that all the friends she had made over the years had made an effort to come and say goodbye.

'It's not goodbye,' she said. 'I'm not so very far away, only an hour by train.'

'Ah,' said Tom, one of the junior surgeons, 'you'll be busy, you'll meet new people! Who knows, you might even get married.' He put his arm round her waist giving her an affectionate squeeze.

Charmian blushed and had to put up with a good deal of good-natured teasing. At last Sister Evans called a halt to the proceedings and made Charmian stand in the middle of the room. This she did with some difficulty as the room was so packed by now. Then she was presented with a parcel, beautifully gift-wrapped.

'Go on, unwrap it, unwrap it,' came a chorus of voices.

Charmian carefully untied the parcel. Inside was the most beautiful ships' decanter in lead crystal.

'I don't know what to say,' she said, 'except, thank you!' She was deluged in a shower of hugs and kisses and good wishes.

It was very late that night, after the party, when she finished packing. Just two trunks and a suitcase. That's me in there she thought, all twenty-five years of me—not much to show really for twenty-five years. For some reason she felt very alone. It was not something that usually bothered her, she was used to being alone. Her parents had both died when she was a tiny child. She had been brought up by a lovable, if slightly eccentric, aunt who had died of old age when Charmian was seventeen, leaving her a reasonable sum of money which Charmian had sensibly invested and never touched, and a few antiques which she treasured.

She was glad to leave her room next morning. Her trunks had been picked up very early and were going down by road. She was going down on the train with just her suitcase to carry. With any luck her trunks would arrive later that afternoon and that would give her the rest of the afternoon and evening to get unpacked. She was anxious to get settled as soon as possible, for that would give her four days in which to explore the town and the surrounding area before she had to start work.

All her arrangements went like clockwork. She arrived on time and let herself into the empty flat with a feeling of suppressed excitement. Her trunks also arrived on time by a miracle of the road transport services and so by ten that evening she was unpacked. Although everything wasn't arranged exactly as she wanted, it was good enough to make the flat feel as if it were hers. She had put her own individual stamp on it. She had put the ships' decanter in pride of place on the coffee table so that the light from the table lamp shone through the crystal, picking up and illuminating the brilliant, sharp-cut edges.

She was standing in the doorway of the lounge admiring her handiwork when there was a knock on her front door. Immediately thoughts of Richard West flashed through her mind and the blood rushed burning to her cheeks. Then quickly she checked herself. This is ridiculous she thought, I've got to open the door and if it is him I've got to speak to him, but I'm not, *definitely* not, letting him in!

The door had a safety-chain which she had fastened and cautiously she opened it to the extent the chain would allow. It wasn't Richard West standing there, and Charmian was annoyed with herself for the momentary small pang of disappointment that flashed through her.

It was John Bourne, the registrar she had seen on her first visit to the Unit. He was small and dark and seemed rather nervous.

'I . . .' he hesitated, 'I share a flat with another doctor upstairs, Martin Challis, he's a registrar in GU surgery.' Another pause while he hopped nervously from one foot to another. 'We wondered whether you'd like to come up for a nightcap now that you've settled in.'

Charmian hesitated just for a moment. 'Not, of course, if you'd rather not,' he added hastily.

'Of course I'd love to,' said Charmian. 'I'd like to start to meet my neighbours.' Grabbing a thick sweater she followed him out of her door and up the stairs. Even with a thick jumper over her T-shirt and jeans she managed to look sexily elegant, a fact which John Bourne and his friend and flatmate Martin, both noticed.

They had obviously gone to some trouble to prepare for a guest. There were candles in red glass holders burning on a low table and dishes with nuts and pretzels by the side, along with an assortment of bottles. Martin, John's friend, was tall and lanky and Charmian guessed they were both aged about twenty-eight. He leaped up when Charmian entered and pulled up a chair for her near the gas fire.

'What would you like to drink?' asked John.

After scanning the bottles hastily Charmian said, 'A dry Martini would be lovely.'

John poured out her drink and brought it over. He smiled shyly. What a nice face he's got, thought Charmian, so gentle. She felt quite at home with these two—she knew they were eyeing her up and down but she didn't feel in the least bit threatened by their attention. She felt rather flattered and completely at ease.

It wasn't long before all three of them were laughing and joking, exchanging stories about the different hospitals they had worked at. To her surprise she found that John and she had both trained at the same teaching hospital in London, St Johns.

'I didn't know that,' said John. 'Although I should have recognised it as soon as I saw you in your uniform. Those frilly caps are always a give-away.'

Charmian laughed. 'Why on earth should you know I was a Johnnys girl? There must be thousands of us and without that special cap I look the same as any other nurse.'

'Oh, I wouldn't say that,' Martin teased.

'Now look here,' said Charmian sternly, 'I hope I'm not going to have to fend you two off, it will be just too exhausting, especially as you are only living upstairs from me.'

John put up his hand in a mock Boy Scout salute, 'We promise, on our honour, we won't make passes at you . . . yet!' he said, and before she had time to reply he added, 'Half a mo,' and dashed out into the kitchen. He came back with three pizzas hot from the oven.

It was well after midnight when Charmian eventually left for her own flat. She had been filled in on a lot of hospital gossip, but apart from a fleeting comment, Richard West's name hadn't been mentioned. Although half of her was dying to know about him, the other half prevented her from letting her interest show. John and Martin obviously didn't move in Richard West's social circle, which was not surprising as he was a consultant and they mere junior doctors. So Charmian had to contain her niggling curiosity, and a persistent niggling curiosity it was. Now that she was back near him, his lean handsome face kept intruding on her thoughts more often than she was ready to admit she liked!

As she was leaving she stopped at the door. 'Thanks, both of you, for making my first evening so enjoyable. It would have been a bit miserable on my own.'

'Well, we are just hoping that you can cook, and that you'll invite us down sometimes,' joked John.

'That's a date,' promised Charmian. 'In the not too distant future, when I know what my duties are going to be, you must come down and visit me.'

Back in her own flat she undressed slowly and showered before getting ready for bed. Sitting at her dressing-table, leisurely brushing her long hair, she smiled at her reflection, thinking of the last time she was in the flat. Thinking of the way Richard West had picked up her long hair and let it slip slowly through his fingers. She wished again that she could have asked John and Martin something about him, but the conversation just hadn't got around to the subject of the head of Intensive Care. Charmian sighed, wishing she could have brought herself to initiate it.

'I thought you weren't going to think about him,' she said out loud, and stared crossly at her reflection in the mirror. She gave her hair a few more strokes, vigorously this time, then picked out a book from the shelf in her room and, climbing into bed determinedly, put Richard West from her mind, concentrating on the book instead. She must have been more tired than she realised because when she awoke in the morning the bedside lamp was still on and the book was lying on the bed, still open at the title page.

The next four days passed quickly, much too quickly. She explored the town, which was pleasant enough with several large parks, all beautifully laid out. The shops, although of course not as plentiful as those in London, seemed just as good and much less crowded.

On her last free day the sun was shining and everywhere outside looked so inviting she decided to explore further afield. She carefully selected a pair of fawn cords and a matching shetland sweater, put on a comfortable pair of walking shoes and then feeling quite like a countrywoman, she caught the bus out to the forest. It had been a king's hunting forest since the eleventh century and one king had been shot there in a hunting accident. Seemingly a very suspicious hunting accident. Charmian made a mental note that she must visit the place, which was now a local beauty spot and marked with a special stone.

The bus journey ended at a small town at the mouth of a river called Hamblington. Charmian fell in love with the little country town immediately. It had one long main street which went down a very steep hill to a small harbour. A jumble of houses and shops of all architectural styles and ages jostled each other for position on the hill, almost as if each one was trying to prevent the other from slipping down the hill to the quay.

At the bottom of the high street was an even steeper, narrow cobbled street that led down and finished at the quay. No cars came here and Charmian felt she was stepping back in time as she strolled down the cobbles and past the whitewashed houses with their baskets, bright with spring flowers, hanging outside in the warm sunshine.

Instead of going for a long walk as she had originally intended, Charmian spent the morning happily rummaging around in the many antique shops which abounded there. When she eventually exhausted those, there were plenty of delightful little shops selling souvenirs for holiday makers. She also found a delicious delicatessen and bought some home-made mackerel pâté. I'll ask John and Martin down for a snack tonight, she thought, tucking it into her handbag.

The sun was really warm by now and Charmian was content to while away some time sitting on one of the seats along the harbour wall, in company with several elderly gentlemen and their equally elderly dogs, watching the serried masts of the many yachts anchored there and listening to the creaking of wood and the occasional flap of a sail. Idly she watched the progress of a very large, sleek, white yacht making its way up-river towards the harbour from the sea. It was under steam, but it was too far away to hear the engine so it appeared to come up-river silently, cutting its way through the milky green water majestically.

There were some children on the prow, excitedly talking and pointing, their clear young voices carrying across the water above the noise of the crying, wheeling gulls and the water lapping on the slipway. Gradually the smooth purr of the engine could be heard and Charmian watched as the yacht turned and expertly berthed at the jetty near the seat where she was sitting. The two biggest children leapt nimbly from the boat and tied the ropes fast to the bollards on the quayside.

She saw a man emerge from the bridge and go down to where the cabins obviously were. He shouted something to the children and they followed him down below. Charmian felt there was something vaguely familiar about the way he walked but couldn't place it. She hadn't heard his voice properly as he was too far away, and the ever present cry of the gulls dominated every sound.

Losing interest in the boat now that it had berthed, she turned her attention to the occupants on the harbour wall. But they all seemed to be asleep in the warm spring sunshine. She sat in the sun a while longer, then decided she would treat herself to a pub lunch before she set off on her travels again. There were several attractive pubs right on the harbour's edge and Charmian chose one that had a bar upstairs, where she could sit on the ledge of the large bow window and look down into the harbour. She could see across and along the river. On the opposite bank the trees came down to the water's edge and the river gradually widened until it merged with the sea. There in the distance she could see the outline of the misty blue hills that she knew must be the Isle of Wight. Her thoughts returned to the white yacht. She wondered whether it had come across from the Isle of Wight, or perhaps it had even come from France.

She ordered some chicken and salad and was sipping a glass of wine when she saw the man and the three children leaving the very boat she was thinking about. They were all wearing faded blue denims, sweaters and yellow sea boots, the sort that tied at the top to keep the water out. They walked across the road towards the pub, the man with a child swinging on each arm and the third child trundling a rather large, fat labrador along behind him. The children were talking animatedly and the man had his dark head bent towards them listening.

Charmian smiled at the delightful picture they made, when suddenly the man lifted his head and with a pang that made her draw in her breath sharply she realised that it was Richard West. He seemed to be looking right at her but she knew he couldn't see her because the sunlight was reflecting off the thick, bottled glass of the bow window. The realisation that he must be married, because they were so obviously his children, made her throat ache with unexpected, unshed tears. She shrank back from the window so that he shouldn't see her and he passed unknowingly by and started climbing the cobbled street winding up the hill. Suddenly it seemed that the sun had lost its warmth and the breeze had a chill to it.

When her lunch arrived she ate it automatically, but it seemed quite tasteless. Try as she would, she couldn't dispel from her mind the haunting image of Richard West's dark, laughing face and the children looking up at him adoringly, so obviously loving him. It was a subdued Charmian who caught the bus back to her flat and prepared her uniform, ready for her first day's duty. She completely forgot the mackerel pâté and her plans for asking John and Martin if they would like to come down.

Much, much later that night as she lay, still sleepless, in bed, she acknowledged to herself that she could so easily have made a fool of herself over the man. For the first time in her life, she realised, a man had stirred her, plumbed deep, sensual emotions within her that she had never known she was capable of feeling. Even with Nick, her fiancé, she had always felt at the back of her mind that there was something missing, some passion he had never aroused in her.

She admitted reluctantly to herself that she had been hoping that he, Richard West, was as attracted to her as she was to him. She smiled wryly to herself. Trust me, she thought. All these years I've thought it would never happen to me! Now it *has* happened and the wretched man is married!

She eventually drifted off into a restless sleep only to be awakened too soon by the ringing alarm clock. After that there was no time to think, only just time to shower, put on her uniform and wrap her thick cloak around her for the walk to the hospital. She walked briskly up the hill towards the hospital in the chilly early morning air, wondering what the fresh day had in store for her.

As soon as she stepped into the Intensive Care Unit she knew it was going to be one of those days. The night staff were still there, sorting out the night's new admissions. John Bourne had been on duty and was there too, case notes piled high on his desk.

'Sorry,' he said, 'but I'm afraid I had to admit three last night, so that means every bed is full.'

The ICU was certainly chaotic that morning, but it was an ordered chaos. Charmian did a quick ward round with John so that he could brief her on the eight patients.

That would prepare her for the proper ward round with a senior registrar who would be arriving at 8.30 a.m. to take over for the day.

'By the way,' said John, 'the boss is away on holiday at the moment and for the next fortnight, so the Unit is being run by Carol Miller, the senior registrar. She will refer on up the line to the Professor if she has any problems she can't handle.'

He stopped by an old man. 'I don't think he's going to make it,' he said. 'We've had him on the blower now for five days,' indicating the ventilator, 'but his blood gases are terrible, and now his urine output is virtually nil.' He gave a deep sigh. 'I think he'll go into renal failure today.'

Charmian felt the old man's pulse—it was weak and she could feel it fluttering wildly.

'I hope he goes peacefully and soon,' said John sadly, 'he was a smashing old chap, used to do the hedges and look after the rose bushes at the tennis club . . . Smashing old chap,' he repeated, looking at him.

'Come on,' said Charmian firmly, steering him towards her office, 'I think it's time you had a cup of coffee and then went home to bed, you're obviously tired.'

'Don't get emotionally involved with the patients you mean!' said John.

'Yes,' said Charmian, 'that's precisely what I *do* mean, and you shouldn't need to be told.'

John allowed himself to be led away. 'I think you are going to be a good sister,' he said, 'but just make sure you always follow your own good advice.'

Carol Miller arrived promptly at 8.30 a.m. and did a very brisk and businesslike ward round. She was tall and good-looking in a hard way and it was evident that she wasn't very popular with the staff. However, Charmian couldn't fault her clinical judgment and she instinctively knew that she wouldn't make the mistake of becoming emotional about patients.

Charmian very quickly got the hang of the routine. The whole unit was very well organised, each patient carefully monitored and the treatment regime constantly reviewed and updated in the light of the patient's response to medication. The staff seemed very friendly—all, that was, except Carol Miller. But as the day was so busy there really wasn't time for social chit-chat and Charmian didn't have the opportunity to get to know her. Carol certainly didn't invite any friendly overtures.

The old man died as John had predicted. Charmian was glad he was off duty. Carol Miller had the task of telling his frail little old wife. Charmian noticed that it didn't perturb her in any way and she couldn't help feeling that she could have been a little more thoughtful and kind in her dealings with the old lady. After Carol had left, Charmian took the confused old woman into the room set aside for relatives and gave her a cup of tea. She called one of the junior nurses in to help the old woman with the necessary form-filling and generally help get her sorted out, telephoning her daughter and arranging for a taxi to take her home.

The bed wasn't free for long. Charmian had no sooner organised the ventilator to be taken off for sterilisation and was getting the empty bay cleaned, when there was a crash call from casualty—an overdose had come in. Carol Miller swore softly. 'If I know that Casualty Officer, the next thing you know he'll be on the 'phone asking us to take the wretched patient.'

'What is the policy here?' asked Charmian. 'Do we or don't we take overdose cases?'

'Only if we have to,' replied Carol firmly, 'and then

only for as short a time as possible. As soon as they can breathe on their own they go back to the ward of whichever firm happened to be on take when they arrived.'

In fact they did admit the case. It was a sixteen-year-old girl who had taken her mother's tranquillisers, a whole bottleful, and it was a very traumatic admission. The mother was with the girl and Charmian found it difficult to keep patience with her. She was overdressed and over made-up. Her only concern seeming to be what people would think rather than concern for the welfare of her daughter. Or perhaps even more important, thought Charmian, why the poor child had done such a thing. The girl was in a deep coma and in respiratory failure. Carol Miller dealt firmly and swiftly with the mother, pumped out the girl's stomach and put her on a ventilator. Charmian admired the way Carol coped with the whole messy situation. She respected her and found that she enjoyed working with her, even if she didn't particularly like her.

One day seemed to merge into another for Charmian and as she was on duty for the weekend it was difficult sometimes to remember which day it actually was! She certainly had no time to miss any of her friends in London. She saw Liz Jefferies only fleetingly when they were handing over duties, but one morning as Charmian was going off duty, the Unit for once was quieter than usual. They actually had five empty beds, so she and Liz had time for a coffee together.

'Is it always as busy as this?' asked Charmian.

'Oh no,' replied Liz. 'You've just hit a particularly bad patch. Baptism of fire as you might say! Anyway I gather you've coped very well.'

'I've done my best,' said Charmian stretching her long

legs out in front of her. 'Mmm, this coffee tastes good! I can honestly say this is the first time I've felt relaxed since I started.'

'Good,' replied Liz, 'then you'll enjoy the party tonight.'

Charmian was surprised. 'What party?'

Liz explained to her that the nurses doing the intensive care course had just finished their exams and they had all successfully passed. So a party had been organised in the seminar room at the end of the corridor, which was far enough away so as not to disturb the patients.

Charmian demurred. 'They haven't asked me,' she said, 'and I'm fairly new here.'

'Rubbish,' retorted Liz, 'they haven't asked you because everyone assumes you are going, and so you are.'

Charmian finished her coffee and stood up. 'Well, I'll see,' she said. 'If John Bourne is going perhaps I'll look in.'

'You do that,' said Liz, 'and if it's still slack here I'll pop along and stick my head in for five minutes myself.'

When Charmian arrived back at her flat she found a note had been pushed through her letter box. *Pick you up at 8 p.m. for the party tonight, John. PS Wear anything you like!*

Charmian smiled. Cheeky devil, she thought, he hasn't even asked me, just assumes I'm going. But she was pleased nonetheless. She had three whole days offduty in front of her and starting off with a party seemed a good omen. First of all, however, she had to catch up on some much-needed sleep. Without more ado she climbed into bed and fell immediately into a deep sleep. She was awakened by a ringing at her door and John's voice.

'I've brought you down a pot of coffee, it's about time you woke up!'

She looked at her watch. Good heavens, nearly two in the afternoon! Hastily wrapping a blue cotton robe around her, she padded barefoot to the door.

'You *are* a pal John,' she said, letting him in.

'Well I really wanted an excuse to find out if you were coming to the party tonight,' admitted John, eyeing Charmian appreciatively.

The blue robe wrapped tightly round her showed off her slender waist and long legs to advantage. Even her tousled hair looked attractive, shimmering silver as it fell about her shoulders. Charmian fetched two coffee mugs in from the kitchen.

'I didn't think I had much choice,' she laughed, 'your note wasn't exactly an invitation, more like an instruction.'

John looked a little uncomfortable. 'I didn't mean it like that,' he muttered.

'I know you didn't,' teased Charmian, 'I'm looking forward to going. Thanks, by the way, for waking me! I should have probably slept on until the party was over.'

She and John sipped their coffee, chatting about the various patients on the Unit. Charmian told him about the sixteen-year-old overdose with the dreadful mother, and the way Carol Miller had dealt with the situation. 'Huh,' snorted John, 'she'll soon be in her element again. Richard West comes back from leave tomorrow and you should see the way Carol throws herself at him.'

Charmian tried to ignore the pulse that beat rapidly in her throat at the mere mention of Richard West's name and made no comment. She had resolutely put Richard out of her mind since the day she had seen him with the children at Hamblington and as the ICU had been so frantically busy that hadn't proved to be too difficult. She wasn't going to let herself fall into the trap of thinking about him incessantly again. Carol Miller could throw herself at a married man if she liked, that was her prerogative thought Charmian, but it's not my style. When I get involved with a man I want it to be without any strings attached.

She didn't bother to pursue the topic with John but gently shushed him out of her flat when they had finished the coffee. 'I've got some shopping to do, and ironing as well, so come down for me at about eight,' she said. 'I'll be ready then.' Clutching his coffee pot John went, albeit rather reluctantly.

Before she knew it the time was seven o'clock and she still hadn't washed her hair or decided what to wear for the evening. She had a hasty shower and shampooed and dried her hair. Opening her wardrobe door she studied its not very extensive contents and tried to decide what would be the most suitable for the evening.

Eventually she chose a sea green, pure silk dress which showed her olive skin off to an advantage, and made the blue green of her eyes even more pronounced. It was sleeveless and perfectly plain and straight. Around her waist she fastened a gold chain and wore gold strap sandals to match. As she usually wore her hair fastened back severely for work, she just brushed it back casually, so that it hung like a shimmering curtain on her shoulders. John couldn't resist a whistle when he saw her, 'Sister Williams,' he said, 'you look ravishing!'

By the time they arrived the party was in full swing. Charmian could see why it was held in the seminar room well away from any patient areas. The noise was deafening. One of the theatre technicians had rigged up a disco complete with flashing lights, and the decibel level of the music must have been equivalent to that of Concorde taking off.

John introduced Charmian to so many people that she soon gave up even trying to remember names, not that she heard many of them anyway! The music was non-stop and swinging and Charmian was never short of a partner for the dance floor. She was dancing with John again when the beat of the music changed to rock and roll.

'Can you jive?' shouted John.

'A little,' replied Charmian, and before she could say anything else she found herself being flung about in rhythm to the music. John proved to be a superb dancer and Charmian gave herself up to the sheer pleasure of the beat of the music and the exhilaration of the dance. She didn't realise that gradually the other couples had drifted off the floor leaving it to herself and John. At the end of the dance when everyone clapped, Charmian suddenly realised that they were alone on the floor and clapped her hands to her cheeks in embarrassment.

'I had no idea you were a dancer as well as a nurse,' said a deep voice in her ear. Desperately trying to control the thudding of her heart Charmian turned and looked into the mocking brown eyes of Richard West. The music changed to a slower, more romantic beat. 'My dance I think,' he said to John and, before Charmian could protest, gathered her in his arms and started dancing. She tried to keep a distance between them, but he would have none of it. His arms were like bands of steel holding her close to him. She felt the warmth of his skin through the thin cotton of his shirt, and against her will her whole body began to tingle in response to the nearness of him.

She stiffened, trying to keep as far away from him as

possible, but the firm persuasion of his hands melted her
flimsy resolve. It was getting near to the end of the party
and someone had turned the lights down very low. As
the lights lowered, so Richard West's arms tightened.
One hand pressed into the small of her back, the other
took one of her hands and put it round his neck. Submissively she let it rest there, not wanting to move it. She
could feel his thighs hard against hers and the nearness
of his body was like a potent drug against which she was
helpless. As she felt his warm breath on her face she
instinctively lifted her head to look at him.

The next moment his mouth came down on hers,
blotting out everyone and everything. Her lips parted as
she responded yearningly to the persuasive ardour of his
searching kiss. A tremor ran through her body as she
clung close to him. She could feel the beating of his heart
against hers as he held her so tightly she thought she
would faint.

Someone switched the lights up and without a word
they broke abruptly apart. His breath was coming in
quick ragged gasps. 'Let's get out of here,' he said
huskily, holding on to her arm tightly.

Panic mounted within her and then Charmian saw
John coming towards them through the crowd and her
fiery emotions began to subside.

'I'm with John,' she muttered, the words sticking in
her throat in her panic and, not daring to look at him
again, freed her arm as she turned quickly and ran across
to John. In the general turmoil of the end of the party she
successfully managed to dodge both John and Richard
West and grabbing her coat made her way quickly out of
the hospital and ran down the road until she reached the
safety of her flat.

Once inside she shut the door and leaned against it

gasping for breath. Her heart was pounding, and it was not just the result of the extra exertion of running down the road. She knew John would be looking for her and felt guilty, but she couldn't face him or anyone at that moment. When later he knocked at her door and asked if she was OK, she just shouted that she had a headache. This was indeed true. She couldn't shut out the memory of Richard's kiss and her body still trembled from his touch. He's married, *he's married*, she kept reminding herself. He's a philandering womaniser, that's quite obvious.

She was glad she had three whole days in front of her before she had to face him again.

CHAPTER THREE

CHARMIAN had some difficult explaining to do to John the next day. She made up a story about a sudden migraine coming on and not wanting to spoil the rest of the evening for him. She wasn't sure whether she had convinced him or not, but he didn't question her too closely or pursue the subject, for which she was heartily thankful. She invited John and Martin down for supper the following evening, as she was still feeling guilty about the way she had left John so abruptly at the end of the party. And she thought that having to go shopping and prepare food would help take her mind off of the subject of Richard West.

Throwing all ideas of thriftiness to the winds, she really went to a great deal of trouble with the meal. Guacamole and crudités to start with—a delicious puree made with avocado pear and yoghourt, with sticks of crisp carrot and celery to dip in the purée. Then, deciding to be adventurous and to try something new, she followed this with veal cooked in sour cream and capers and served with plain boiled rice and a tossed green salad. For dessert she made her own favourite raspberry mousse with fresh cream, to be followed by coffee, mints and brandy. It made a sizeable hole in her housekeeping allowance, but she felt she owed John and Martin something for their kindness to her.

As she was working in the kitchen that afternoon it occurred to her that Liz was probably off duty that evening, and on an impulse she rang through to the ICU on the internal hospital telephone which was in her flat.

'Intensive Care Unit,' said a voice, 'Dr West speaking.'

Not that she needed to be told, the sound of his voice sent tremors racing through her and it took Charmian a few seconds before she could compose herself in order to speak coolly.

'I wanted to speak to Sister Jefferies,' she said, not mentioning her own name in the vain hope he wouldn't recognise her voice.

'Certainly, Sister Williams,' he said. She thought she detected a hard edge to his voice. 'I take it, by the way, that you got home safely after the party?'

'Yes thank you,' she answered primly, praying that Liz would come quickly to the phone, so that she couldn't be forced into any compromising explanations. To her relief he said nothing else, but she had a mental vision of his dark lean face with those firm, chiselled lips set in a hard line.

It was with relief she heard Liz come on the line. 'What is it, love?' she asked.

Charmian explained that she was cooking dinner for Martin and John and wondered if Liz could come too. 'Please come, Liz,' she finished.

'Don't you think I'm a bit long in the tooth for you young people?' queried Liz.

'Not a bit of it,' said Charmian. 'I'd love you to come, and besides, you can give me your honest opinion of my cooking.'

'Well, OK if you insist, yes I'd love to come,' answered Liz, sounding pleased. 'Now let's see, I get off duty at six this evening, say about six thirty after I finish handing over to Staff for the night. So would about seven thirty at your place be all right for you?'

'Great,' Charmian replied and was just about to put the phone down when Richard West's voice came over the line.

'How about asking me?' he said.

'I don't think it's quite your scene,' Charmian replied coldly, suddenly angry with him for pushing himself onto her. What a nerve that man had! Perhaps he was thinking she was willing to have an affair with a married man! Well, she'd soon squash that idea.

'I suggest you go home to your huge family for dinner!' she snapped and with that she slammed the phone down.

Her wrath made her resolution to put him out of her mind easy as she carried on with the preparations for the evening meal. When Liz arrived the table was set, the ships' decanter was filled with as good a sherry as she could afford and she had set out her best lead crystal glasses by the side of it. The glasses and decanter glittered and sparkled in the lamplight. As she was pouring Liz a sherry Charmian explained that the decanter was a gift from the staff at her previous hospital, and that the glasses were in fact antiques and had been left to her by her aunt.

'Good heavens,' laughed Liz, 'I'm almost afraid to drink from them. You had better tell those boys when they arrive to be careful. Martin in particular, as he seems to have two left feet. How he manages to perform surgery I'll never know! I always think it is just as well the patients are fast asleep!'

They both laughed and sat in easy companionship either side of the low table sipping their sherry. Liz eyed Charmian curiously for a moment and then said, 'I don't know what it was you said to Richard on the phone after you had spoken to me, but whatever it was, you had him rattled!'

Charmian stared into the golden depths of her sherry, absently twisting the glass so that little points of fire flew from the sharp edges of the cut glass.

'Good,' she said quietly, but the undercurrent of venom in her voice had not gone unnoticed by Liz.

'I do hope you two are going to get on,' she said in a worried tone of voice. 'He really is a very nice man you know.'

Charmian raised her eyes. 'I'm sure he is an excellent doctor,' she replied non-committally, 'and that is all I'm interested in.'

It was just as well John and Martin arrived at that moment because Charmian felt sure Liz was going to quiz her about that cryptic remark. However, once they had arrived there was plenty of noise and laughter and no opportunity for a tête-à-tête, for which Charmian was very grateful. The dinner party went off perfectly, and everyone agreed that Charmian was a cook *par excellence*.

'I don't know how you do it,' remarked Liz, sitting back contentedly. 'All this cooking, and you still somehow manage to look unruffled and glamorous.'

'Yes,' agreed John. 'You'll make some man a marvellous wife someday. At the end of the day you'll be there with a sumptuous dish ready that you've spent the whole afternoon preparing.'

'My aim in life is to make a career for myself,' said Charmian, 'and not to spend it slaving over a hot stove for some man!'

'Oh God,' groaned John in mock horror, 'I wish Women's Lib had never been invented.'

'It was not invented,' retorted Charmian hotly. 'It has evolved.'

'All right, all right,' said John hastily. 'Pax, pax!'

'Well,' said Liz, quietly bringing the conversation back to an even keel, 'a career is one thing. Sometimes it is possible for a woman to combine both, sometimes not. One thing I will tell you though, and that's that a career only is a lonely life.' She reached over and squeezed Charmian's hand, 'Just you remember that, my girl.'

Much later in the evening as they sat with their coffee and brandy, talk invariably turned to hospital gossip. John and Martin knew all the latest love affairs and scandals and took great delight in recounting them all. Charmian felt her cheeks beginning to burn. Had anyone seen that passionate kiss at the end of the party? She fervently hoped not.

When John started talking about Carol Miller and Richard West, half of her felt relieved because they obviously didn't suspect her of having any romantic notions about him. The other half felt hurt when she heard Carol and Richard's names being linked together. Curiosity got the better of her and she began to pump John gently with questions, first about Carol, hoping to lead on to the subject of Richard later.

'Carol!' exploded John. 'My God, she's an absolute man-eater. I can understand why that husband of hers divorced her.'

'Carol, divorced?' echoed Charmian. 'She doesn't seem old enough to have been divorced.'

'How old do you have to be?' rejoined John cynically. 'Anyway, I gather they got married when they were both medical students. He is a surgeon now and she's an anaesthetist—the two don't mix very well.'

'I think she's only a "man-eater" as you call it,' said Liz, 'in order to prove something to herself. Perhaps she was badly hurt.'

'I suppose you could be right,' admitted John grudgingly, 'but she's always setting her cap at some man, and at the moment it happens to be Richard West.'

'Does he,' said Charmian as calmly as possible, 'set his cap at her?' She felt she had to find out something about Richard's character. Was he really as bad as she suspected? If so, why on earth couldn't she just dismiss all thoughts of him and have done with it!

'I think,' Liz interrupted firmly, 'this conversation should end now, before we tear everyone's reputation to shreds!'

She made Charmian sit down with another brandy and organised John and Martin into clearing up the table. Then tying a tea-towel around each of their waists, she set them to get on with the washing-up.

Charmian grinned. She could hear Liz gently chiding them about the thoroughness, or lack of it, in their cleaning and tidying. She treats them like her children, she thought. She would have made a good mother. Suddenly Liz's words earlier in the evening came back to her—a career only, is a lonely life. Cupping her hands around the balloon of the brandy glass she swirled the translucent golden liquid around, wishing she could see into the future. What did it hold for her?

Her reverie was disturbed by Liz coming back into the room, followed by John and Martin. 'I must be going now,' said Liz collecting her things. 'Thank you for a lovely evening, and congratulations on your cooking once again, it was a marvellous meal.' She kissed Charmian on the cheek. 'Now don't sit there all night talking with these two,' she indicated John and Martin.

'Don't worry, we'll go with you,' said John. 'We're both on duty, unfortunately, at the crack of dawn tomorrow.'

As they were leaving John turned to Charmian at the door. 'By the way, I'm off the day after tomorrow. How about a trip to Winchester, it's a lovely city, I know you'd like it.'

Charmian didn't want to commit herself, she felt instinctively that John was getting too attached to her and was unsure of how to put him off without hurting his feelings. So, thinking quickly, she said, 'Can I let you know tomorrow night? I'm waiting for a call from a friend in London.' She crossed her fingers behind her back as she told the white lie. 'I've promised if she is free I'll meet her.'

John looked disappointed, making Charmian feel guilty. 'Well, I hope your friend can't make it,' he said.

Charmian slept in late the following morning. She had not bothered to set her alarm and was still soundly asleep when the ringing of the front door bell aroused her.

'Just a moment,' she called sleepily, and slipping into her blue robe she splashed some cold water on her face to help wake herself. Picking up her hairbrush she walked to the door and opened it, still brushing her hair. She stopped, brush poised in mid-air. It was Richard West.

'I thought I'd come and see how my new Sister was settling in,' he announced to her amazement, walking past her into the lounge.

'I . . . er, I'm not dressed for visitors,' said Charmian feebly, cursing herself for opening the door and letting him walk straight in.

'So I can see,' said Richard slowly, his gaze lingering on the swell of her breasts with the hint of her small, pointed nipples jutting through the thin cotton of her robe. A hot colour suffused her cheeks and self-consciously Charmian pulled her robe tightly around her and put one arm defensively across her breasts.

'I seem to remember you were not such a shrinking violet the other night at the party,' he said mockingly, a cynical smile curving his chiselled mouth.

'It was just a . . . a party kiss, if that is what you are referring to,' said Charmian defiantly. 'I shouldn't let it give you any ideas.'

He stepped towards her and grasped her by the shoulders. The heat of his hands seemed to burn through the thin cotton of her robe. 'Was it?' he said thickly, 'was it just a party kiss?'

Charmian put up her hands defensively to push him away, and even through the smooth material of his tailored suit she could feel the iron-hard muscles of his chest.

'Hey, do you mind!' he said suddenly, his mouth crinkling at the edges with laughter. Charmian realised that she had the prickly hair brush in her hand and was prodding him in the ribs with it.

Somehow it broke the ice and brought her back down to earth. He seemed less threatening and she no longer felt quite so vulnerable. Breaking away from him swiftly she said, 'I don't know to what I owe the honour of this visit, but if you will wait a moment I will change and make you a coffee.' Then she added with an emphasis he couldn't mistake, 'Before you leave.'

She fled into the bedroom quickly before he could reply and changed after bolting the door. Better safe than sorry she thought. She threw on a pair of dark blue cotton, baggy pants with a blue Indian cotton top in a slightly paler shade. Tying her hair back swiftly into a pony-tail she went into the kitchen to make the coffee.

'Do you take your coffee black Dr West?' she called.

'I'd prefer it if you called me Richard,' he said. 'I

intend to call you Charmian.'

He wandered nonchalantly into the kitchen and leaned on the fridge top, drumming his long fingers, watching her make the coffee with an indolent challenge in his eyes.

'And before you get on your high horse, Miss Williams,' he mocked, 'I would inform you that everyone in the Unit calls each other by their first names, so I don't see why you should be the exception . . . *Charmian*.' As he spoke her name he gave an intimate ring to it.

'OK by me,' said Charmian, coolly avoiding his eyes. Putting the coffee-pot and two cups on a tray, she carried it through to the lounge. As she passed him he made no effort to move but, defiant, she gave no hint of her raw nerves and brushed past him in the narrow confines of the doorway.

She passed him a cup of steaming coffee with trembling hands, hoping he wouldn't notice the spoon tinkling in the saucer as the cup wobbled precariously. She found his presence unsettling enough and his silent scrutiny even more so.

'Well,' she said at last, after sipping her coffee slowly, 'I asked you before—to what do I owe the honour of this visit?' Her blue eyes fringed with heavy dark lashes looked coolly into his, not betraying the fact that her nerves were vibrating in an alarming manner.

'Why did you run away at the end of the party?' he asked, coming directly to the point.

'It was the end of the party. I just decided it was time to go, that's all,' replied Charmian, knowing full well that it was an inadequate excuse. But her mind seemed incapable of functioning clearly with this man sitting so close to her. Anyway, she thought mutinously, why should I have to make excuses? I haven't done anything wrong!

He put down his coffee cup suddenly, and swiftly moved in one lithe movement from his chair to her side on the sofa. 'You little liar,' he hissed in her ear. 'You were afraid of your own emotions go on, admit it.'

He put his hand lightly on the nape of her neck, running his long fingers up into her hair. Her breath caught in her throat, the touch of his hand making her painfully aware of her vulnerability.

Gathering together all her will power she stood up. Looking down gave her a momentary sense of having the advantage over him. 'I think you have read more into that little incident at a party than is warranted.' Her voice sounded brittle and unreal in her ears. She felt angry that this man should have the power to awaken this response in her. Her anger gathered strength; he was so damned sure of himself! The sensuality in his voice and in his eyes when he looked at her made her all the more determined to control the unfamiliar sensations he aroused. 'I don't know what your relationships are with other women colleagues in the hospital, or elsewhere for that matter,' she said icily, 'but I can assure you that I am most definitely not on the market for an affair!'

With that, Charmian haughtily stalked across to the door and with admirable aplomb opened it. Although inwardly shaking she managed to maintain a calm exterior. Richard West seemed to hesitate.

'Have I not made myself clear?' snapped Charmian, vehemently driving her point home.

Richard moved across the room to the doorway, his face dark with anger. 'Yes,' he said harshly, 'you have made yourself abundantly clear.' He turned at the doorway and gripped her roughly by the hair at the back of her head, pulling her pony tail hard so that her head tipped back and she was forced to look into his dark, smouldering eyes.

'I've got some interesting information for you too,' his voice grated harshly. 'You lead men on the way you do and you will find out the consequences the hard way—and I can guarantee you won't like it!'

Abruptly he let go of her, adding menacingly, 'Perhaps that's really what you want!'

'Get out,' whispered Charmian furiously, 'get out of my flat.'

'Certainly,' he almost snarled at her in his anger. Then he left, slamming the door so hard the wall shook with its reverberations.

Charmian leaned against the door, her breath coming in shallow, rasping gasps, burning-hot tears pricking her eyelids. How unfair and cruel he was! She hadn't run after him, *he* had made all the overtures! She had responded, it was true, but she hadn't been able to help herself, damn him! She knew about men like him. His only intention was to use her. He already had everything he wanted, a family, and probably every woman he met falling at his feet. That is if they all behaved like her! She wished she could have gathered her wits together more quickly and answered him back, but he hadn't given her the chance. Clenching her fists she thumped the closed door with her small hands, releasing the pent-up frustration.

'I hate him, I hate him,' she muttered through clenched teeth, 'I hate him!'

Then misery overwhelmed her and bursting into tears she flung herself on the sofa, burying her head in the cushions, sobs racking her slender body.

CHAPTER FOUR

FOR CHARMIAN the day dragged on interminably and miserably. She polished and cleaned every single item in her flat with an energy born of suppressed anger and frustration. When, later in the evening, John rang to ask whether she had made up her mind about Winchester the next day, she said yes immediately, she would love to go. Actually she had completely forgotten about his invitation, but she'd also forgotten her previous misgivings and, thinking that anything would be better than sitting around moping or being by herself, she seized the opportunity of company.

Getting ready the following morning, for once not in a tearing rush, she took out a flamboyant red dress from her wardrobe and put it on. Her reflection stared back at her from the mirror.

'The scarlet woman,' she said out loud and laughed bitterly. Then she sighed. 'I wish I was,' she whispered, 'then I could have an affair with Richard West and it wouldn't bother me at all.'

The dress was slim and figure-hugging and had a short jacket with a full swirling back. She had bought the outfit in a mad, reckless moment and had never since had the courage to wear it. Today though, it suited her mood. She felt aggressively defiant and reckless. But in the deep recesses of her mind she did feel some nagging, guilty doubts about accepting John's invitation. I'll just have to be careful not to let him get the wrong idea, she told herself.

When she opened the door to John there was no doubt how he felt about the red dress. He beamed from ear to ear.

'You look great,' he said. 'Absolutely great.' And taking her arm, a mite too possessively for Charmian's liking, he escorted her to his car.

She was amazed to find that his car was a brilliant yellow Lotus. A gleaming roadster, sleek, smooth and streamlined, and very low and difficult to get into as she soon found out! Charmian had to admit that she enjoyed driving along in the startling yellow machine, and both she and the car got plenty of admiring glances from passers-by.

'I must say I'm surprised at your choice of car John,' she said. 'You are such a quiet person, I thought you would have a . . .'

'A sedate sort of car,' interrupted John grinning. 'Well you see, underneath every quiet chap there's a wild, dashing cavalier trying to get out.' He pulled a comical face and Charmian laughed.

They were stationary at some traffic lights at the time, and suddenly without warning John leaned across, put his arm tightly round her and planted a firm kiss on her lips. Then he released her just as suddenly and put the car into gear, ready to go when the lights changed.

'John,' Charmian protested, 'please, there are other people and cars about.' As she spoke she glanced at the car that had drawn up at the side of them at the traffic lights. It was a large dark blue saloon. Charmian looked sideways up at the driver, hoping he hadn't seen the stolen kiss. To her horror and chagrin she saw Richard West looking down at her, his lips set in a straight, narrow line. She knew with certainty that he had seen that kiss. Her cheeks stained bright pink with embarrassment, but flashing defiant fire from her blue eyes she tilted her head proudly and looked forward. But not quickly enough to miss seeing the line of his jaw tighten and the sardonic rise of his eyebrows.

The lights changed and John stabbed his foot on the throttle and the car roared away. He had been quite unaware of the occupant of the next car and Charmian saw with relief that Richard West's car turned left at the next junction.

In spite of the unfortunate episode at the traffic lights and the spectre of Richard West's face glowering down at her, Charmian enjoyed her day in Winchester. The weather was perfect and John knew the city well and was an interesting guide.

Charmian loved the traffic-free High Street, with its uneven flagged paving stones. On one side the shops were under an arcade supported by Doric-style pillars, and looking up the length of the High Street towards the castle at the top of the hill gave her the feeling that she'd gone abroad for the day. The effect was definitely continental.

John agreed. 'I always think looking towards the Butter Cross,' he indicated an ancient market cross set high with stone steps encircling it, 'that Winchester seems to have an almost Bavarian influence.'

Charmian could see what he meant, but walking through the passage-way by the Butter Cross into a quiet square and then through to the Cathedral close, the atmosphere changed. It just couldn't have been more English. The trees had the translucent green haze of their tender new leaves about them. The grass of the close surrounding the massively solid, grey stone cathedral was the brilliant green of an English spring. An air of peace and serenity pervaded the whole scene. They walked leisurely round the entire close. John turned out to be quite knowledgeable about architecture and pointed out to Charmian the different types of houses and their ages. Many were built in the traditional Wessex style with flint-stone walls. He took Charmian into one of the tiniest churches she had ever been in, dedicated to St Swithin.

At first she had had no idea where they were going. John just suddenly said, 'Come on,' as they were walking through a magnificent ancient gateway which led out of the cathedral close, and taking her arm he steered her across the road to where there was another archway. At the side of the arch there were some very steep wooden steps. 'I know you'll like this,' said John, and when they reached the top he stood back and let her see for herself.

'You're right, I do!' said Charmian softly.

The church was minute and absolutely plain. Rough cast whitewashed walls and ancient beams criss-crossing in a series of arches overhead. The only decoration in the entire little church was a simple arrangement of white and yellow flowers on the altar, lit by a shaft of sunlight filtering in through the uneven leaded windows. The other colour was provided by the intricately worked tapestry cushions neatly hanging over the back of each simple wooden seat.

'I should never have found it on my own,' she said turning to him. 'You seem to know Winchester very well indeed.'

'I ought to,' said John, 'I was born here.' He smiled, 'I'm what you call a Hampshire Hog—that's a nickname given to people born and bred in Hampshire,' he added by way of explanation.

After walking some more they had lunch in the garden of a pub by the river. The river was swiftly flowing at this point and there was an ancient water-mill near by. Sitting in the warm spring sunshine, with the constant splash and rush of water in the background, Charmian felt luxuriously relaxed. She sighed and stretched.

'Oh, this is the life,' she murmured. 'Just think, this time tomorrow . . .'

'Don't think about tomorrow,' said John. Reaching over he took her hand and raised it gently to his lips. 'Let's just enjoy today.'

Charmian felt a lump in her throat. Dear John, she didn't want to hurt him. Gently she withdrew her hand.

'John,' she began awkwardly, 'I . . . I don't know how to say this, but . . .'

'You're not very keen on me,' he interrupted and she could see the disappointment written on his face.

'No, no it's not that. I like you very, very much,' said Charmian desperately searching for the right words. 'But I don't want you to think there is more to our friendship than there is. I don't want you to do something silly, like fall in love with me.'

'It may be too late for that,' said John quietly, looking down studiously at his hands.

'Please, John, can't we just be friends?' She touched his arm pleadingly. 'I do need you as a friend. Can't we try and keep it that way?'

John looked up, his large brown eyes looking troubled. 'Is there someone else then?' he asked.

Charmian hesitated, not knowing what to say. The fact that the someone else was Richard West, that he was married, forbidden fruit, didn't really make any difference. She knew at this moment that her heart, whether she liked it or not, belonged to him.

'Yes,' she answered, her voice so low that John had to lean forward to catch her words, 'there is someone else and I . . . I can't talk about it. I'm sorry, John.' She raised her eyes in mute appeal. 'Forgive me.'

John looked into her face, then he sighed. 'All right, I'll never mention it again. From now on I'll try to regard you as my sister. It won't be easy, but I'll try.' He stood up, 'I think I need another drink.' Picking up the empty glasses he strode back into the pub.

Charmian sat looking at the green-flecked water rushing past. She was glad that things had come into the open between John and herself, but she couldn't help wishing that she could have felt differently towards him.

John was as good as his word—the perfect gentleman. They finished their sightseeing trip of Winchester by climbing to the top of St Giles' Hill. It was a steep hill with steps zigzagging to the very top, from where there was the most marvellous view of Winchester and the surrounding water-meadows. John pointed out to Charmian the lines of the ancient medieval ditches that were still to be seen draining the meadows.

In the evening they went out into the country to a little French restaurant called 'La Chaumiere', which served the most delicious food. It was very late when they finally arrived back at the flat. At her front door Charmian turned.

'Thank you, John, for an absolutely perfect day,' she said.

John's gentle face looked a little sad, 'Thank you for coming,' he said, and taking her hand brushed it very lightly against his lips.

When she finally fell into bed Charmian found she was aching all over and completely exhausted. She hadn't realised Winchester was so hilly!

The ringing of her telephone awoke her next morning. Sleepily she picked it up and murmured, 'Hello?' The next moment she was wide awake as if she had been douched under an ice cold shower.

'Are we to be graced with your presence this morning?' enquired a coldly sarcastic voice at the other end of the line.

Charmian glanced at the clock. Oh God, it was gone nine and she should have been on duty at eight thirty! She must have forgotten to put on the alarm!

'I'm sorry,' she stammered. 'I . . . I must have overslept. I'll be right there.'

'The ward round will start in ten minutes,' Richard West's voice barked down the phone ominously. 'Be there.' The line went dead.

For a split second Charmian sat in bed paralysed. Then it was as if a tornado had hit the flat. How she managed it she didn't know, but she was in the Unit in nine and a half minutes flat looking as neat as ever, except for a few wisps of hair that were escaping from her cap.

She tried to apologise for her lateness but Richard West curtly brushed her explanations aside, giving her no opportunity even to speak. He proceeded straightaway with the ward round, conferring at length on each case with Carol, who had shot Charmian a disdainful look when she had rushed, puffing and red-faced, into the Unit. She proceeded to stay close to Richard looking like the cat who had stolen the proverbial cream.

When he wanted information from the nursing side he made a point of asking one of the junior nurses and completely ignored Charmian from start to finish. By the end of the round she was seething. There's no need for him to be so damned rude, she thought. She gathered up the patients' notes, and resisting the urge to hit him over his arrogant head with them, took them back to her desk. She needed to read through each set of notes to catch up on the events of the past three days, to familiarise herself with each new patient and their treatment regimes, and also to see what progress the old patients had made.

It was about eleven thirty in the morning and the Unit had settled down a little. Most of the pathology specimens had been collected and sent off to the lab. Carol Miller was busy doing the blood gases on a couple of patients, so Charmian sent two of the junior nurses off for a coffee break. About a minute later Richard came over to Charmian.

'I need to put up a central line on Mr Jenkins,' he said curtly, indicating a frail old man in the corner. 'He's so emaciated he hasn't got any decent veins to speak of, so I'm doing it myself, and I shall need your assistance. Please get everything ready for me.'

I suppose I should be thankful he said please, thought Charmian indignantly as she put down the notes she was halfway through and got up from her desk.

'Yes, sir,' she answered evenly. But he didn't even wait to see if she had heard, just swept back into his office without another glance.

Charmian called Bill, the intensive care technician, and between them they set up a trolley with a selection of cannulae and Charmian set about preparing the patient. She was gently swabbing down the skin with alcohol to sterilise it where the needle would enter, when Richard West's voice called her.

'Sister,' he said, standing at the foot of the bed.

'Yes?' she replied, carrying on with her task.

'Come here,' he barked. The other nurses and Bill looked up curiously.

'When I ask you to assist me I expect you to take the

trouble to follow my protocol.' He pushed the trolley away. 'I do not use any of these. I use the latest thin wall cannulae because there is a reduced risk of vein irritation. Surely you know that in a patient such as this it is essential to minimise every risk?'

Charmian flushed. She felt humiliated in front of everyone. 'I'm sorry,' she said as evenly as she could, 'I didn't realise there were any others in stock.'

'As sister on this Unit you should make it your business to know exactly what we do and do not have available,' he snapped. 'But perhaps your hectic social life takes precedence and precludes you from taking an active interest in the unit!'

Charmian opened her mouth and was about to fly back at this unfair comment with a sharp retort, but then thinking better of it bit her lip and let the remark go unchallenged.

She wheeled the trolley into the room where all the stores were kept, Bill following her. With trembling fingers she cleared the trolley and asked Bill where the latest cannulae, that Dr West wanted to use, where kept.

'I don't know,' he whispered, frantically looking in all the trays. 'I don't know what he's talking about.'

Richard West appeared in the doorway.

'By the way, Sister,' he drawled arrogantly, 'you will find the cannulae in question in the top right-hand drawer of my desk. They are a new sample batch I am trying out!'

Charmian drew a deep breath and counted to ten slowly. Then with her blue eyes flashing sparks, she tried to go past him towards his office. He made no effort to move out of the doorway to let her past, so she pointedly waited a moment. She was damned if she was going to squeeze past him! They could both wait there all day as far as she was concerned. At last he stepped back, and as her angry eyes met his she saw mocking laughter lurking there.

After that episode Charmian tried to make sure that he had no cause to reproach her for anything else, but it seemed that he was bent on criticising her and was not pleased with anything she did. Somehow he managed to find a million and one things that he wanted altered or changed in some way. He was splitting hairs, she knew that. She also knew that he was waiting for her to lose her temper and flare up, and she was determined she was not going to give him the satisfaction of seeing that he had rattled her in any way.

'Certainly, Dr West,' she said and smiled frigidly, as he brought her some patients' notes in which the pathology reports had not been clipped in properly. 'I shall get it seen to immediately.'

He stood there glowering. 'I cannot tolerate anything that bears the hallmark of sloppiness,' he growled.

'I quite agree with you,' Charmian responded sweetly. 'I shall speak to Nurse Andrews, she should have done them this morning. However,' she added firmly, 'she is new to the Unit and we all of us have to learn.'

She bent her head back to her work in a clearly dismissive gesture. This day can't end soon enough, she thought bitterly, stabbing her pen viciously into the Kardex index she was updating.

It was a long spell of duty that day and it was early evening when, as she was sitting at her desk talking to a patient's relatives, Richard West and Carol Miller came by.

'Goodnight, Charmian,' he said. Charmian looked up, surprised that he should call her by her first name in such a friendly fashion after being so positively hateful all day. A flicker of annoyance passed over Carol Miller's face.

'Come on,' she said, 'we shall be late.'

Richard didn't move, but stood looking at Charmian as if waiting for her reply. Then he said briefly, 'Make sure you are on time tomorrow!'

'I shall,' Charmian replied stiffly. She wasn't going to be caught out like that again! 'Goodnight, Dr West.'

He opened his mouth as if about to say something but then, realising the visitor was taking an inquisitive interest in the conversation, he turned on his heel without another word and walked down the corridor with Carol Miller. Charmian saw her clinging to his arm as soon as they were a few yards away.

She was glad to hand over to Liz Jefferies who was coming on that night. She felt emotionally and physically drained. Liz tried to persuade her to stay and have a coffee with her but Charmian declined.

'You look all in,' said Liz sympathetically, 'Has it been a bad day?'

'You could say that,' replied Charmian. But although Liz was evidently curious she didn't bother to elaborate on her statement. She knew the other staff would gossip about the way Richard West had treated her. Liz would know soon enough!

Although the spring days were now becoming very warm it was still cold at night. Charmian wrapped her thick cloak tightly round her as she walked out through the pool of light at the hospital main entrance and into the chill darkness of the night. She took a short cut through one of the car parks. It was only when she was halfway through that she realised how badly it was lit. The overhanging trees were thick and cast dense black shadows. She quickened her step nervously and looked back over her shoulder. Was it her imagination, or was that a sound behind her? So intent was she on looking back over her shoulder that she cannoned straight into the man standing unlocking his car door.

A strangled gasp of fear escaped from her as she stumbled and fell against the car. Two strong arms held her tightly. Charmian raised her slender hands and vainly tried to push the dark stranger away. She tried to scream, but no sound came from her paralysed throat.

Suddenly a torch light was flashed on her face.

'Charmian!' said Richard West's voice. 'What the hell do you think you are doing walking through here alone? You could get raped, or worse still, murdered!'

At the sound of his baritone voice her terror subsided. Indescribable relief flooded through her being. She leaned gratefully against him.

'Oh, thank goodness it's you!' she breathed. 'I thought . . . well, I don't know what I thought. I was so frightened.'

Richard opened the car door, 'Get in,' he said, 'and slide across to the passenger seat.'

Charmian didn't have the energy or will to argue, she just did as he ordered. Richard slid his long form into the driving seat beside her.

'My home is quite near here,' he said. 'I'll take you there for a drink, or a coffee if you prefer, then I'll drive you back to your flat.'

Charmian gave a rueful grimace in the darkness. Typical of the man! In spite of everything, he just assumed that she would do as she was told! Almost as if she had spoken out loud he suddenly turned to her.

'Unless, of course, you have a prior engagement.' There was an edge to his voice almost challenging her to dare to have other plans.

'My only plans were to have a quiet evening,' she said. 'But I thought you had an engagement with Carol Miller?'

Richard laughed. 'That, my dear girl,' he said, 'was a very boring, but fortunately short meeting of the Medical Finance Committee.'

He spun the car out of the hospital grounds, down the road past Charmian's flat and headed north out of the city.

'We didn't get granted the funds for the equipment we asked for,' he added.

Charmian couldn't resist a sly dig. 'I thought you *always* got what you wanted!'

He turned to face her briefly. 'I do,' he said softly. The tone of his voice sent danger signals shivering through her. It seemed to imply that he was not referring to medical equipment alone. From the glow of the streetlamps as they flashed past she could see his mouth curved in a slight smile.

She sat in an increasingly awkward silence. She didn't want to meet his wife and family, but at the same time she wanted to be with him.

At last, plucking up courage, she said, 'It's very kind of you, rescuing me, for want of a better word, in the car park. However,' she carried on hastily before he could interrupt, 'I don't think I ought to impose on your family at this hour. Your wife must be getting dinner.'

His response was totally unexpected. He threw back his head and let out a great roar of laughter, simultaneously swinging the car into the drive of a large house. Still laughing, he drove around the house to the back, where a door was illuminated by an old-fashioned swinging gas-lamp.

Stopping the car in the soft gravel of the drive he

turned to her, still laughing. 'Who the hell have you been talking to?' he asked. 'I am a bachelor, not married.' He leaned across to her. 'Not even divorced!'

He got out of the car and walked round to the passenger side to open the door for her. As she got out he deftly slipped an arm round her waist beneath her cloak.

'I'm a bachelor,' he whispered in her ear, the warmth of his breath making her senses reel. 'And I've lured you back to my lonely house!'

The tip of his searching tongue outlined her small shell-like ear. 'I must, in all fairness, tell you that I have the most evil intentions!' His voice has a teasing note to it, challenging her to react.

Charmian swiftly manoeuvred herself out of his grasp and reach. 'I think I would have been safer in the car park,' she said sharply.

She knew somehow she had to keep control of herself and the situation she now found herself in. The fact that he was not married was singing sweetly through her mind, but a little nagging voice of doubt was telling her that the reason he was not married was that he was so damned attractive he could have any woman he wanted!

Richard turned as he was putting the key in the lock. The lamp swinging overhead cast a dark shadow on his face, obscuring her view, but she could tell from the sound of his voice that he was suddenly serious again.

'Getting back to the car park,' he said. 'Don't let me catch you, or rather don't ever do such a damn silly thing again.'

'I can look after myself,' answered Charmian defensively.

Richard said nothing, just raised his eyebrows expressively as he opened the door, switched on the lights and ushered her into a beautiful, pine-clad kitchen.

Everything was in immaculate order, with work-tops gleaming. It was *too* immaculate, thought Charmian, looking around. It almost had a clinical air about it.

He slammed the door shut behind him and stepped across to Charmian. 'Can you really look after yourself?' he asked. 'Would you like me to put that statement to the test?'

Charmian backed nervously away.

'Well,' he said mockingly, then suddenly his dark eyes were crinkling at the edges and she could see a hidden smile lurking in their deep, dark depths.

'Don't worry, you are not going to have to prove it to me.' He came towards her and gently slid her cloak from her shoulders, but made no attempt to caress her. Charmian didn't know whether she was pleased or disappointed!

'Come into the lounge,' he said and led the way through to a large room, subtly lit and tastefully furnished. The furnishings and paintings on the walls were the bare minimum needed, but a feeling of opulence was added by the fact that most of the furniture was antique and all of it in pristine condition.

Charmian felt out of place in her hospital uniform. This was a room for an elegant woman. She noticed, however, that she wasn't the only creature out of place. Stretched out on a comfortable Victorian button back sofa, in a somnambulent posture was the dog she had seen with Richard and the children at Hamblington.

'Is that your dog?' she asked.

The dog opened one eye lazily, inspected her, decided she was of no further interest and went back to sleep.

'That's Hector,' answered Richard. 'Believe it or not, he is supposed to be a guard dog!' He went across and pulled his ears affectionately. 'He's feeling a little disgruntled at the moment—he's missing the children.'

'The children?' queried Charmian.

'My sister's. They've been staying with me here, I've been teaching them to sail.'

So that explains that, thought Charmian. I really ought not to jump to conclusions.

Richard went over to the drinks cabinet at the side of the room. 'Now, what can I fix you?' he asked.

Charmian hesitated for a moment, the cabinet was filled with every bottle imaginable. Richard, however, didn't wait for her answer but disappeared into the kitchen and came back a few moments later with a bottle of champagne.

'We'll have a champagne cocktail,' he said. 'My favourite drink. Do you like them?'

'I've never had one,' confessed Charmian.

'Well there's a first time for everything,' he laughed.

He made two enormous cocktails and came across to Charmian, handing her a glass of bubbling liquid gold.

'To?' he said, raising his eyebrows questioningly.

'To our friendship,' replied Charmian, trying to look him firmly in the eye with difficulty.

She sipped the champagne. The bubbles made her want to sneeze.

Richard watched her. 'Come on,' he said, smiling. 'Let's sit, we might as well be comfortable while we drink.' He led her across to an elegant *chaise longue* on the other side of the room.

CHAPTER FIVE

CHARMIAN twirled the champagne glass uneasily in her fingers. The sugar frosting on the rim caught the light and reflected the golden glow of the liquid. Little granules of sugar falling from the rim into the champagne sent up a myriad of tiny golden bubbles, racing to the surface.

Richard was seated close beside her, his eyes never leaving her. There was subtle seduction in every glance and Charmian was having to fight hard to resist the irresistible. His suave charm was slowly but surely enveloping her senses.

But even so, she was unsure of herself. Why had he invited her back? That little nagging voice was telling her he was too confident of his powers of attraction. He had treated her despicably all day and then, when he was ready, he had changed his mood and obviously had no doubt that she would be compliant.

She sipped the champagne and almost reluctantly raised her eyes to his, afraid of what she might see. Over the rim of his glass his dark quizzical gaze met hers.

'Well,' he said. 'Do you like it?' nodding at the cocktail in her hand.

'It's very good,' said Charmian, 'but perhaps hardly the drink after a hard day's work and on an empty stomach.'

'Then that's a good reason for me to invite you out to dinner,' replied Richard.

'I'm not dressed for dinner,' Charmian indicated her uniform.

'No,' agreed Richard. He slid an arm along the back of the *chaise longue*, letting his hand rest lightly on her shoulder. Charmian had to swallow hard to ease the strangling sensation in her throat. The mere touch of his fingers sent ribbons of fire throbbing through her veins. She knew that if he put his arms around her she was in no mood to resist. Her tiredness, the champagne and the closeness of his body to hers all combined, robbing her of her free will, drugging her in a cloud of physical desire.

With a momentous effort Charmian steeled herself, dragged her reeling senses together and moved slightly away from him.

'I think I would like to go home now,' she said.

'Why, are you afraid I might seduce you?' he mocked.

'I'm not the type to be seduced,' she retorted angrily, resorting to sharpness as a means of defence, 'and I'm most certainly not afraid of you.'

'Then why do you want to go?' persisted Richard.

'I'm tired,' said Charmian. 'It was a busy and somewhat difficult day.' She flashed him a meaningful look. Had he completely forgotten his behaviour towards her during the day?

His lips curved in a sarcastic smile. 'You think I was unreasonable!'

'I don't think, I know!' snapped Charmian. 'And now, if you don't mind, I really must be going.' She stood up.

Richard leaned back, casually crossing his long legs. 'But we still have over half a bottle of champagne left,' he said. 'It seems a pity to waste it.''

'You must find someone else to share it with you,' Charmian said firmly. She walked across to the cocktail cabinet and replaced her glass there. 'May I go now?'

After just a fraction of a second's hesitation Richard leapt up and, placing his glass besides hers, led the way through to the kitchen. Charmian followed thankfully. He said nothing at all but the line of his jaw was hard and unyielding and his hooded eyes masked whatever he was thinking.

He locked up the house, opened the car door and ushered Charmian into the car, all the while saying nothing. During the short drive back to her flat the silence that reigned between them was so brittle that Charmian felt as if it could have been physically snapped. She felt as if she were sitting on the edge of a volcano, never knowing when it would erupt and, worse still, not knowing what would happen when it did!

When they arrived at her destination he braked the car abruptly. Charmian put out her hand to open the door. 'Thank you for the drink,' she said in a tightly controlled voice. 'I am . . .' but her words were lost as Richard's mouth came down on hers, claiming her lips in a bruising punishing assault. There was nothing tender about his kiss. It was relentless and hard, his tongue prizing her lips apart and searching out hers with a devouring bitter sweetness. Charmian let out a little moan, partly from the pain of his arms gripping her so tightly and partly from the bitter ecstasy he aroused. At the faint sound Richard abruptly let her go,

'Goodnight,' he said thickly, and reaching across flicked the door open for her.

With shaking limbs Charmian climbed out of the car and stumbled up the path to her flat. In a daze she heard Richard's car roar away into the night. He must have pushed the accelerator pedal straight down onto the floor, judging by the speed at which he left.

A tumult of contradictory emotions welled up in her as she fumbled to get her key in the door. Anger, love, hate, desire . . . Which was predominant at that moment was impossible for her to tell. Once inside she took off her uniform and threw it violently into the laundry basket, getting rid of some of her pent up emotions. This is ridiculous, she told herself. This man is manipulating you as if you are a puppet on a string!

Still giving herself a severe mental lecture on her foolhardiness and stupidity, she ran a bath. Common sense told her to lie back and try to unwind. But it wasn't easy, there were so many unanswered questions.

Why had he been so hateful to her all day? Why had he then taken her back to his home? Why had he kissed her like that? Charmian sighed and restlessly swished the scented bubbles around the bath. There was no doubt that he was as sexually attracted to her as she was to him. Although for him she was certain that was where it stopped. In other words *lust*. He knew he had aroused her and had assumed they would make love, but she had called a halt.

Charmian wished she was more worldly, like Carol Miller. Because of her sexily elegant appearance everyone assumed that she had been involved in love affairs. But Charmian had inherited some old-fashioned ideas from her aunt and knew that she wanted to be in love, and to be loved, before she gave herself to any man. It had never been hard to resist any man before, but Richard West's compulsive masculinity made it very difficult. How she was going to face him the next day she didn't know.

In fact, the next two days turned out to be relatively easy as far as working with Richard West was concerned. He was preoccupied with three American doctors, visiting the Unit. He was charming and businesslike and his involvement with the Americans kept him out of her way most of the time. Charmian was very glad. She had been dreading facing him, but she was pleased and flattered when he asked if she could look after the three Americans for a whole day, to give them the benefit of an English nursing sister's knowledge and expertise, as he put it.

Also the fact that Carol Miller was sidling up to him at every opportunity worried Charmian less than she thought. At least it takes his mind off me she thought, and that in turn means I don't have to worry about how I feel for him!

She couldn't help watching a little forlornly though, as the two of them walked out together late one evening. Carol was talking earnestly and Richard had his head down, as was his habit, listening intently. Watching him walk with his head bent, listening, reminded her of the day she had seen him with the children. She sighed. Why can't we get on better, she thought miserably. We're either quarrelling or nearly making love!

However, she didn't have a lot of time to reflect on her tangled emotions where Richard West was concerned, even after the Americans had left. The Unit always seemed to be busy and Charmian was too much of a professional to let her personal problems intrude into her work. In the hospital, patients came first and foremost and as there was a constant flow in and out of the unit, the days passed miraculously quickly.

Charmian gradually got to know the other nurses better. Most of them were unmarried and quite a few were living with their boyfriends. They used to tease Charmian good-naturedly about the lack of a man in her life, and one day when she joined them for coffee break she found they had organised a little surprise for her. Three of the girls had decided that it was about time they fixed Charmian up with a man. They had written out a long list of eligible bachelors and pinned it on the wall. When she came into the room they grabbed her and blindfolded her.

'Hey, what's happening!' protested Charmian.

'Just you wait and see,' said Jane, a lively young staff nurse who was always up to pranks. She put a large drawing pin in Charmian's hand.

'Now,' Jane said, 'we are going to twirl you round three times and then you must put the pin in the chart.'

'And then?' queried Charmian laughing.

'We've cast a spell,' they giggled, twirling her round. 'The man whose name you stick with the pin will automatically fall in love with you!'

Ignoring Charmian's protestations of 'rubbish', they pushed her forward with shrieks of laughter and Charmian duly stuck the pin in the chart.

'How about me falling in love with him?' she asked as she pushed in the pin. 'Isn't that important?'

'I didn't think you were the falling in love kind,' said a deep voice with a Scots twang behind her.

Charmian ripped off the blindfold. Richard West had obviously been watching with amusement from the doorway. He strode over and looked at the list of names.

'I see I'm the lucky man,' he said raising his eybrows. 'Look where you've stuck the pin.'

Charmian stared in disbelief. She had stuck it bang in the middle of Richard West's name. It hadn't even occurred to her that the girls would have dared to have put his name there.

'I can't guarantee that their spell will work of course,'

he said. 'But it will be interesting to find out.' His eyes burned searchingly into hers.

'We were playing a childish game,' said Charmian self-consciously, 'and you were quite right. I'm not the falling in love kind.'

With that she swept out of the room and back to her desk on the Unit, anything to get away from his electrifying presence as quickly as possible. She tried to concentrate on the notes in front of her, but the words and figures swam crazily out of focus and although she tried to ignore the fact, she was very conscious of his tall figure approaching her desk. But he didn't stop, just walked straight past, tying on his mask as he went. He called Bill and asked him to get some fresh plasma from the fridge, then together they went into the cubicle of a young man who had been in the unit for twenty four hours. He was eighteen years old and suffering from multiple injuries as a result of a motor cycle accident.

Charmian had the boy's notes on her desk and realised that Richard would almost certainly need them, so picking them up she took them across to him.

'You'll be wanting these,' she said, and hung them on the clipboard at the foot of the bed.

'Thanks,' said Richard. He was putting up another drip on the boy and Charmian admired the gentle, deft way he slid the cannula into the vein on the back of the boy's hand.

'Come and meet Stephen,' he said, 'now that he's conscious. You've had quite a nasty crack on the head, old man. Along with quite a few other bumps and scratches.'

He was chatting to the boy all the time, gently coaxing the story of the accident out of him. Stephen's pale face began to show signs of interest as he haltingly tried to tell his story. His confidence in Richard was evident, as was the extreme pain he was suffering whenever he restlessly made the slightest movement.

'Now, this is Charmian,' said Richard reaching out his hand to grasp hers and draw her near. 'She is going to get you ready for theatre this afternoon. That's why you are having another transfusion now.'

Stephen's bottom lip trembled and for a moment Charmian thought he was going to burst into tears.

'Don't worry about a thing,' she reassured him gently. 'The sooner the orthopaedic surgeons fix those legs of yours, the sooner you'll be out of hospital.'

'I'm going to leave you now with Charmian,' said Richard. 'And I can tell you young man, a good many men would like to be left to her tender mercies!'

Charmian looked at Richard, his head bent in that familiar attitude he had, his mouth curved in a now gentle smile, his eyes twinkling encouragement at the boy. Stephen smiled wanly and transferred his gaze reluctantly to Charmian as Richard left his bedside. She called for one of the nurses to assist her and Jane came over.

'Sorry about the pin business,' she whispered as she helped roll the bedclothes back. 'I hope he wasn't angry?'

'Not at all,' answered Charmian briskly, 'he hasn't mentioned it. He took it for the joke it was. Now, we've got to get this young man ready for theatre this afternoon.'

Together they gently prepared his broken legs, wiping off the congealed blood carefully, cleaning the whole area again, making the surface wounds as clean as possible.

Charmian rang the anaesthetist and arranged for him

to come down and examine Stephen pre-operatively and write up the premedication.

'He's rather apprehensive,' she told him. 'Dr West has given the all-clear, together with the neurosurgeons, and as there is no cerebral damage he says he can have any premed you think fit.'

The anaesthetist wrote Stephen up for a fairly strong premedication and Charmian stayed with him until he gently drifted off into the relaxed euphoria that a good premedication gives. When he had gone to theatre, she decided to catch up with her paper work before going off duty. She was absorbed in preparing duty rotas for the next batch of intensive care course nurses, due to start the following week, when the crash call came.

Carol came out of Richard's office clutching her bleeper and grabbed the telephone. Charmian heard the telephonist's voice requesting an anaesthetist immediately in Casualty.

'On my way,' said Carol briefly and started running out of the unit and down the corridor in the direction of Casualty.

CHAPTER SIX

CHARMIAN carried on with her work on the rotas. It was quite a problem getting all the girls sorted out, making sure they all had adequate opportunity for clinical practice, as well as organising their study and lecture days.

She sighed. It seemed that no sooner than she had organised one batch of lectures than the wretched doctors all found something absolutely imperative to do at the precise time they should have been giving their lecture. This meant a complete rearrangement of the schedule, involving many lengthy telephone calls. Wearily Charmian plodded on until she thought she had eventually cracked it, then she threw down her pen on the desk and leaned back with a satisfied sigh, glad to have finished that boring job. Paper work was one part of a sister's duties she did not enjoy, it was so unrewarding. She enjoyed patient contact.

Looking at her watch she saw it was a quarter of an hour after she should have finished. She had been so busy with her rotas that she hadn't noticed how late it was getting nor, come to think of it, how late the night staff nurse was in coming on duty.

Charmian smiled wryly. One thing, she thought, I shan't jump down her throat, I know what it's like to be late! While she was waiting she busied herself packing away her papers in the drawers of her desk. The phone rang and swiftly Charmian picked it up.

'Intensive Care, Sister Williams speaking.'

'Oh Charmian,' it was Carol's voice on the other end of the line. 'Is Richard still there? I want to talk to him about admitting this patient I'm with in Casualty.'

Charmian fetched Richard who came and listened intently to what Carol had to say, saying, 'Yes,' abruptly now and then.

Putting the phone down at last, he said to Charmian, 'We shall be admitting another patient. Is the side ward, room four, available?'

'Yes, it is,' answered Charmian, 'but isn't it rather far from the nursing station for a new admittance? We usually put the newest patients where we can see them from here.'

'I know the policy, Charmian,' replied Richard.

Charmian flushed, put in her place again! Of course he knew the policy, so why should there be a different procedure this time?

It seemed that Richard was reading her thoughts because he said, 'This isn't quite our usual type of admission.'

Charmian raised her eyebrows expressively as she tied on her mask and prepared to receive the new patient. Wasn't the usual type! What on earth was he talking about?

Staff still had not arrived on duty, but Charmian didn't worry unduly. Besides, her curiosity was aroused and she willingly stayed on to organise the admittance of the new patient herself.

The doors to the Unit opened and the patient came in on a trolley wheeled by two porters. Carol was with them holding a saline drip up as they walked along. But it was the crowd that followed behind them that caused Charmian to gasp. There were at least ten people, all talking and crying at once and the noise was deafening.

Even Carol had lost her usual cool, calm air and was looking decidedly hot and flustered.

Charmian rushed forward. 'I'm afraid this is as far as you can come,' she said firmly. The unruly mob surrounded her and Charmian noticed that they all seemed to be excessively made up, even the men! However there wasn't time to puzzle over it, she just concentrated on steering them firmly back in the direction from whence they had come and somehow, marvellously, she managed to escort them all into the visitors' waiting-room.

Charmian had to shriek almost to make herself heard above the constant babble.

'Please wait here, and please be *quiet*!' She shouted the last word and it had some effect on her listeners. She continued in a more normal tone of voice. 'Dr West will be here to answer your questions as soon as possible. Until then please be quiet.' She lowered her voice and her audience looked at her, dramatically quiet by now. 'There are many very sick people here. I know you will think of them and be as quiet as possible.'

She backed out of the room, glad to get away from her strange audience. There was something about them, something she couldn't quite put her finger on. As she hurried back into the Unit she smiled to herself, they certainly were a strange lot, almost like circus people.

Little did she know at that moment how near she was to the truth. They were in fact members of a ballet company. The patient Carol had asked to be admitted was the male principal dancer, Anton Kiminski. He had been taken suddenly violently ill during a backstage party, and had been rushed to Casualty in a state of collapse. That had accounted for all his friends being made up. They were all still wearing their stage make-up!

She found out that much in the short space of time it took her to go down the corridor from the visitors' room into the main area of the unit. Jane had come rushing up to her excitedly whispering all the information she had been able to glean.

She finished off by saying, 'He's fantastically good looking!'

'Just you keep your mind on your job!' retorted Charmian sharply, but her smile belied her words. She was curious herself, and even more anxious to find out what catastrophe could have brought a famous dancer like Anton Kiminski into the Unit.

Having sent Jane off to organise some physiotherapy for another patient, Charmian went across to the side ward. Inside the room Richard was standing there with Carol. The handsome young man in the bed was on a ventilator and was unconscious. Charmian waited for a moment for her instructions, then Richard glanced across at her.

'We have quite a severe case of anaphylaxis here,' he said, 'unless I'm very much mistaken. He has been given an antihistamine injection and is now on a ventilator as you can see.'

'How long do you think he will need to stay on it?' asked Charmian, looking at the dancer lying so still in the bed. Jane was right, he was fantastically handsome. Even though he was unconscious and on a ventilator and looked terribly ill, it was impossible to miss his striking good looks.

'Shouldn't be too long I hope,' replied Richard. 'We'll keep him on until the oedema subsides.' He handed Charmian a scribbled list on the hastily made up notes.

'These are the tests I want run on him as soon as possible, and could you find out which physician is on take tonight.'

He turned back to Carol, deep in conversation while looking anxiously at his patient. Charmian returned to her desk and picked up the phone.

'Oh, switchboard,' she said to the operator, 'can you tell me which firm is on medical take tonight?'

'Dr Pickard,' came the reply over the phone.

Charmian popped her head into the ward and told Richard. He and Carol were still standing by the bedside in deep conversation.

'Thanks,' said Richard.

'Do you want me to get him for you?' asked Charmian.

'No,' said Richard. 'I'll ring him myself. I want him to come down and give a second opinion on this young man.'

Charmian went back to her desk to ring the duty registrar, but she needn't have bothered. As she put the phone down from bleeping him he came into the Unit. Charmian didn't know him very well as he had only just arrived at the County General, but he seemed hard-working and pleasant.

'Sorry, Dick,' she said as she handed him Richard's scribbled list and the patient's notes. 'I'm afraid there's quite an evening's work for you already, and you only just started!'

'You can say that again,' said Dick looking aghast at her through his spectacles. 'What is wrong with this guy anyway?'

'A severe case of anaphylaxis according to Dr West,' replied Charmian, 'but he is asking Dr Pickard to come down and give a second opinion.'

Dick opened his eyes wide, 'Is that all?' he said. 'I thought by all that racket back there,' he waved a hand in the direction of the visitors' room, 'that there had been a murder at least!'

'Dick!' remonstrated Charmian. 'I think it's quite bad enough, you shouldn't joke about it.'

'Sorry,' muttered Dick looking a little shamefaced, 'it's just that I can't stand histrionics.'

Charmian sighed. She had forgotten about the people who had accompanied Anton Kiminski to hospital. She must remind Richard to go and speak to them. He still hadn't come out of the patient's room, so she went across to remind him. He and Carol came through the door as she arrived.

'I told the people who arrived with Mr Kiminski that you would speak to them,' she said.

Richard scowled. Carol had obviously primed him on how excitable and noisy they were.

'I'm sorry,' said Charmian apologetically, 'but they did seem rather anxious. Well, *very* anxious to be exact, and I thought you could set their minds at rest.'

'Oh, you did, did you?' replied Richard sternly, then he smiled and the depths of his dark brown eyes lightened and sparkled. 'All right, deliver me to the lion's den. Theatrical people always terrify me,' he remarked as they walked down the corridor.

'You surprise me,' Charmian couldn't help replying. 'I didn't think you would be afraid of anyone.'

'Oh, I am,' said Richard, pausing to push the door open for her. As she passed through the door he caught her wrist in his strong warm hand. 'Even you frighten me sometimes.'

'Me?' stammered Charmian, acutely conscious that

his nearness was having a devastating effect on her—as usual.

'Yes, *you*,' he said in a low voice. 'Particularly when those big blue eyes of yours flash dangerously, as they do when I have annoyed you!'

'Don't annoy me then,' returned Charmian as flippantly as she could in spite of her thundering heart.

'I'll try not to in future,' said Richard releasing her wrist.

Charmian darted in front of him, leading the way to the visitors' room. Her face was flushed and she knew it. That man! one word from him and she was reduced to a quivering wreck!

She left Richard with the room full of Anton Kiminski's friends and made her way back to the Unit. By now she was beginning to feel tired and her stomach was sending out loud signals of hunger. Where was staff? Surely she should be here by now? Charmian looked at her watch. It was nearly ten and she should have been off duty at six.

Jane came up to her as she arrived back at her desk.

'The Night Nursing Officer has asked me to stand in for staff tonight,' she said, a pleased expression on her face. 'Staff is sick, so I'm to act up.'

Charmian frowned. 'That means you will be one short here tonight,' she said slowly. 'I think you are going to be too busy, Jane.'

'No, no, we'll manage,' said Jane quickly. 'Another nurse from one of the wards has been sent in, and she's done some intensive care work in another hospital.'

Charmian hesitated. Jane was enthusiastic but rather inexperienced and a trifle impetuous. She wondered whether everything would be all right if she was left in charge.

'Look,' said Jane impatiently, 'you are due off duty and I can manage. I'm not a baby—I *am* an experienced nurse you know!'

Charmian smiled, 'All right. The experience will do you good. If you run into any problems you *will* call for help won't you?'

Jane sighed and rolled her eyes heavenwards. 'Do you really think I'm going to be left alone much? Dr West is going to be buzzing around this unit until everything has settled down. You know that.'

Charmian laughed, she knew that was true. 'OK, you win,' she said. 'I'll go now and I'll see you in the morning when I take over.'

Jane practically hussled her off the unit, fetching her cloak and opening the door for her, she was so anxious to be left in charge! Charmian walked home wondering whether or not she had done the right thing. Although common sense told her to stop fussing, she realised she had no choice anyway—she was due back on duty herself in the morning.

Once home she suddenly found she was very tired and was glad to throw off her uniform and relax with a book in her houserobe. As usual these days, when she was not busy her thoughts were drawn back to Richard West. Her mind readily conjured up a vision of his dark, brooding good looks. She relived and savoured the memory of the two kisses he had given her and wondered if he had any inkling of the way he made her go weak at the knees. I wonder what he really does think of me, she wondered sadly. If only I could make him go weak at the knees!

She shook her head, half smiling, at such a ridiculous notion. Richard going weak at the knees for anyone! He only had to snap his fingers and any woman would be glad to go running she thought, including me!

She sat on the settee, a small, slim figure hugging her knees, her silvery hair tumbling in disarray on her shoulders. You must get him in perspective, she told herself fiercely. He is just a very attractive man who maybe, only maybe, likes you a little. Remember, casual kisses mean nothing to most men she told herself, don't read something into his actions that isn't there.

'*So* Charmian Williams,' she said out loud. 'Stop thinking about him, stop dreaming about him and get a hold of yourself before it's too late!'

She completely ignored the persistent little voice at the back of her mind telling her that it was almost certainly too late anyway, and went to bed determinedly thinking of anything and everything except Richard West.

Jane rose from the desk to greet her in a very efficient and businesslike manner the next morning. Everything was meticulously in place and the unit was functioning in its usual competent manner.

'Well?' asked Charmian. 'How did it go?'

'I'm going to work hard and become a sister in an Intensive Care Unit,' announced Jane. 'I have decided I like being in charge.'

Charmian laughed. Evidently all had gone well. 'Tell me about the patients,' she said.

Jane briefed her on the events of the night and worked her way methodically through the patients' notes, coming eventually to the last one, Anton Kiminski.

'Oh yes,' remarked Charmian, picking up his notes. 'Still on the ventilator is he?'

'Is he by heck!' replied Jane, letting her efficient sister-type mask slip and relaxing back into her normal impulsive self. 'He wasn't on that damn thing for more than three hours! He seems to be completely recovered.'

'Good, I'm glad to hear it,' said Charmian.

'Well, I'm warning you,' said Jane, leaning forward and whispering confidentially, 'don't turn your back on him. Talk about Russian romantics! He has the worst case of roaming hands of any man I've ever met. I've always thought ballet dancers were . . . well, you know! *He* most definitely isn't!'

'If he's as well as you say he'll be leaving this morning,' said Charmian gathering up the notes, 'so he won't have much opportunity for his hands to go roaming!'

'He doesn't need much opportunity,' replied Jane.

'And I'm afraid he's not leaving, anyway not just yet,' said Dick gloomily joining them. 'Dr West has ordered a whole host of tests and he's got to stay here until we've run them all.'

'But surely,' protested Charmian, 'that's a waste of a bed on the unit?'

'If we were full up, yes,' replied Dick. 'But as we're not at the moment, there's not much we can do about it. The on-take medical firm had a very busy night last night, so their ward is full and they can't take him.'

'Oh well,' said Charmian, 'I'll just have to remember your advice Jane, and not turn my back on him!'

She worked her way round the patients, clipping their notes back on to the bottom of their beds, stopping to have a brief chat with Bill, the technician, before crossing to room four with Anton Kiminski's notes in her hands. According to the notes he had suffered a severe reaction to food. It seemed that Richard West and Dr Pickard suspected lobster but couldn't be sure. That was why he was having more tests before he was discharged.

Although Jane had said he was completely recovered, Charmian wasn't prepared for the change in the young man in room four. He leaped off the bed with athletic grace and swept Charmian into a waltz before she was aware of what was happening.

'Mr Kiminski, please!' she gasped, struggling out of his embrace, her cap askew and the ties of her gown flying open at the back.

'This is a hospital you know, and you are supposed to be a patient.'

'Where have you been all my life?' he said quite unrepentantly with a trace of a foreign accent.

'If you will get back into your bed and lie down,' Charmian said firmly, 'I will take some blood from you. Dr West has ordered some more tests.'

'Tests! Tests!' he moaned. 'I am well. I don't need any more tests.'

'Dr West thinks otherwise,' replied Charmian. 'Now, please lie still.'

He patently couldn't stand the sight of blood as he kept his face averted and his eyes tightly shut while Charmian gently slid the needle in his arm to withdraw the dark red venous blood. As soon as she had the samples she needed, she swabbed his arm and stuck a sticky plaster on firmly.

'You can sit up and open your eyes now,' she said, 'it's all finished.'

Anton sat up and looked at her with admiration in his eyes.

'You didn't hurt me at all,' he said wonderingly.

'I should hope not,' replied Charmian. 'I'm trained not to hurt patients.'

Suddenly Anton reached up and, before Charmian could stop him, pulled her cap off and drew her down so that she was sitting on the bed. 'What is a beautiful girl like you doing working as a nurse?' he asked.

'Because I like it,' replied Charmian. 'Thank you for the compliment, however.' She tried to rise but he laughingly held her there. Charmian struggled a little more determinedly and tried to grab her cap from his hand. But he tantalisingly dangled the cap just out of reach and, leaning over the bed trying to catch it, Charmian lost her balance and ended up in a heap in his arms. It was at that precise moment that Richard West walked in.

'Sister!' he exploded.

Anton released his hold on Charmian, who extricated herself from his arms with lightning speed, blushing a brilliant red and wishing the floor would open up and swallow her.

'I know Mr Kiminski is better, but I don't think he is quite *that* well, Sister!' Richard's voice was amused.

Charmian didn't dare look at him, she knew she was dishevelled, her hair had fallen down, her gown was undone and her skirt had ridden up over her knees. Half-heartedly she tried to tidy herself up but it hardly seemed worth the effort, for she knew she must be looking such a mess. She felt stupid and annoyed with herself for letting Anton Kiminski get the upper hand.

'I er, I . . . ,' she began.

'You can tell me later,' cut in Richard. 'I would suggest you go and tidy up now. I shouldn't like any of the junior nurses to see you!' He picked her cap up from the floor where Anton had dropped it and handed it to her.

Charmian snatched it from him angrily. She was angry with herself and with him for laughing and also with Anton Kiminski for putting her in such a ridiculous position. Richard courteously held the door open for her, laughter brimming his dark brown eyes. He was rewarded by a withering glance from Charmian as she stalked out of the room with as much dignity as she could muster in the circumstances.

Later on that morning when she had cooled down sufficiently to be able to tell the other girls what had happened, she was able to laugh at herself.

'I think you were very lucky to be in his arms,' said one of the junior nurses. She sighed dramatically. 'He's the man of my dreams.'

Charmian snorted. 'You don't want to dream about a man like that! He's the kind of man who is after every woman that comes near him. You should dream about a dependable type.'

'But they're not exciting,' the young nurse rejoined. 'I want a man who will sweep me off my feet.'

'And deposit you in a miserable heap somewhere?' retorted Charmian briskly. 'Oh no, my dear, take my advice and steer clear of that type of man.'

'What type may I ask?' said Richard, joining the group having coffee in the rest room.

'The womanising type,' said Charmian quickly, 'like Anton Kiminski.' She was tempted to add *and you*!

'Perhaps the sight of you drove him mad with desire!' observed Richard, a strange smile curving his lips.

Charmian felt herself blushing again at his strangely intimate gaze and hoped the other girls wouldn't notice. She drained her coffee cup quickly and put it down.

'I must be getting back to my post,' she said, standing and smoothing her uniform.

It was a signal for the other girls to go also and they rinsed their cups and stacked them at the side of the little sink. Charmian refilled the automatic coffee-pot, which was nearly empty, before she left. Richard sat in one of the easy chairs watching her, not speaking. She was very conscious of his eyes on her and wished she had left the job of replenishing the coffee-pot to somebody else, but having started it she had to finish it. She started to leave the room.

'Oh, Charmian,' came Richard's voice. 'I wanted to have a quick word with you about our famous patient.'

She paused in the doorway suspiciously. Was he going to bring up that embarrassing incident again? 'What about him?' she asked.

'I've decided he can leave this afternoon. Can you arrange for someone to pick him up and organise that Dr Pickard and I see him in a week's time when the results of all his tests will be through?'

Charmian nodded. 'Yes I'll do that right away.' As she started to leave Richard added,

'By the way, I should get one of the others to go into the room with you as you seem unable to control him!'

'Don't worry, I shall control him,' said Charmian grimly. 'If necessary over my dead body!'

'I shouldn't like to see it come to that,' said Richard softly, his voice filled with laughter. 'I suggest you need a chaperon.'

Charmian looked at him sharply, her blue eyes puzzled. He was laughing at her and yet he seemed to be half serious. What was he thinking? Did he really think she couldn't manage that particular patient? Well, she thought ruefully, I suppose I didn't give a very good impression last time.

'I will take your advice,' was all she said as she left to return to her post.

The rest of the day passed smoothly, very smoothly considering what a riotous start it had got off to! Anton

Kiminski had apologised profusely when Charmian had returned to his room. She did take along another nurse for moral support, but his behaviour was exemplary and he appeared very penitent. Charmian couldn't help liking him. He was attractive in a wicked sort of way, like a small boy caught with his fingers in the jam-pot, thought Charmian.

'You will come and see me dance?' he asked Charmian.

'I would love to,' she replied, 'if it is possible.'

'It will be possible,' said Kiminksi decisively. 'I shall *make* it possible.'

Charmian laughed. 'You are impossible,' she said.

After he had gone, escorted out by a bevy of friends, the unit returned to its usual quiet routine. The buzz of excitement that he had generated subsided and every-one went about their dutes as usual. Charmian finished her tasks and was clearing her desk ready to leave when Liz arrived.

'What's all this I hear about you capturing the heart of a famous ballet dancer?' she asked.

'I don't know what it is you've heard,' replied Charmian laughing, 'but you can be sure it is greatly exaggerated.'

'It's the talk of the hospital,' said Liz. 'At least it will be if Jane gets her way.'

'Jane wasn't even here,' said Charmian. 'She's just picked up a bit of gossip second hand from one of the other girls.'

She started to collect her cloak from the locker outside the staff room, still chatting and laughing with Liz when Jim, one of the night porters, came along carrying an enormous basket of red rosebuds.

'What gorgeous roses,' said Liz bending down to

sniff their delicate fragrance. 'One of the patients is lucky.'

'It isn't one of the patients,' said Jim. 'Sister Williams here is the lucky one.'

'Me!' said Charmian startled. 'Whoever would be sending me roses?' For one wild, sweet moment she thought they might be from Richard, then common sense told her not to be so stupid. What on earth would he send her roses for, and even if he did, would he send them to the Intensive Care Unit? She bent down and took the ticket from the side of the basket. In very fancy handwriting with lots of scrolls and flourishes it said:

> To Juliet from Romeo
> To the Sleeping Beauty from her Prince
> To my Beautiful Charmian from Anton.

Charmian smiled. What a mad man he was! 'It's from the ballet dancer you were hearing about,' she said to Liz.

Liz's eyes nearly popped out of her head. 'I thought you said everything was greatly exaggerated!' she exclaimed.

'He evidently *was* driven mad with desire at the sight of you!' Richard's sarcastic voice cut through Liz's enthusiastic oohs and aahs over the flowers.

'Just because a man sends me flowers doesn't mean anything,' said Charmian stiffly, disconcerted by Richard's presence.

'Well it means something when *I* send them,' he said firmly. 'Not that I do very often.' He bent down and picked up the basket.

'Would you like me to give you a lift home? It will be difficult walking with this huge basket.'

'No thank you,' replied Charmian quickly. 'I shall put them in the visitors' room. They can be appreciated by everyone there.'

'You'll do no such thing,' gasped Liz absolutely horrified. 'It isn't every day a girl gets red roses, and it's even less often that girls get red roses from an international star! You must take them home with you.'

So, reluctantly, Charmian had to accept Richard's offer of a lift. He made a great point of carrying the roses at arm's length as they walked down the hospital corridor, much to Charmian's annoyance and the amusement of the rest of the staff.

CHAPTER SEVEN

CHARMIAN was glad when they reached her flat and Richard pulled the big car to a halt.

'Thank you for giving me a lift home,' she said politely, climbing out of the car. 'Don't bother to get out, I'll take the roses from the boot myself.'

'It's no bother,' answered Richard already out of the car. 'Anyway, I thought perhaps you might invite me in for a coffee. It's been a long day.'

Charmian hesitated, remembering the last time he came in for coffee. She didn't want to invite him in, his presence was too disturbing to her and she was terrified that she would betray her true emotions to him. What would he do if he knew that she was finding him harder and harder to resist?

Watching his bent head as he retrieved the roses from the boot Charmian reflected that perhaps it was true, that old wives' saying that love was closely akin to hate. She itched to run her fingers through his crisp, dark hair and to feel the outline of his clean-cut jaw.

'Well?' asked Richard, disturbing her riotous thoughts. 'Am I to be asked in for a coffee or not?'

'All right,' said Charmian, feeling she didn't really have any alternative but to ask him.

'Now that's an invitation I can't resist,' said Richard sarcastically. 'You're so enthusiastic you've bowled me over!'

Charmian had to laugh. 'Well, you haven't exactly

97

given me a lot of choice and I've had a long day too, you know.'

'I know,' Richard cut in quickly, 'so why don't we go out for a meal? We can have a lazy evening.'

'No thank you,' Charmian answered, desperately trying to think quickly of a plausible excuse. She intuitively knew that it would be putting too much temptation in her path too soon. She knew that her resolve to withstand Richard West's attraction was all too flimsy. 'I have quite a few things I have planned to do this evening. Things I really must do. But thank you anyway for asking me.'

Richard didn't pursue the matter, for which Charmian was thankful. He just waited while she searched feverishly through the contents of the bottom of her bag for her key.

Once inside she quickly put on a pot of coffee while Richard made himself at home and sat with his feet up on her settee. While waiting for the coffee to perk she started putting the roses into a vase.

'I wasn't joking when I said he must have been driven mad at the sight of you,' said Richard, watching her.

Charmian flushed uncomfortably and manoeuvred herself so that her back was turned to him as she finished putting the roses in water. 'Rubbish,' she said firmly.

'You are an extremely attractive young woman, surely you must know that?' Richard's voice said softly near her left ear. His large, strong hands rested lightly on her shoulders.

She twisted quickly away out of his reach, unable to stand the pleasurable tingle the touch of his hands brought. Wishing more than ever that she had had the strength of mind not to invite him in, she moved to the kitchen to fetch the coffee. Richard followed her and leaned against the doorway as she loaded the coffee-pot and cups onto a tray.

'Could you get me the milk out of the fridge?' she asked coolly. Anything to take his eyes off her so that he wouldn't see the trembling of her hands. Richard obliged and Charmian carried the tray through to the lounge.

Attempting to try to keep the conversation on the subject of work, a topic on which she felt safest, Charmian asked, 'Do you really think Anton Kiminski was violently allergic to lobster?'

'It seems to be so,' answered Richard, taking the proffered cup from her. 'Do you know, I've never seen such a violent reaction to food, although I have read of it of course.'

'Yes, but what made you plump for lobster?'

'Simple,' answered Richard. 'He had lobster at the stage party. He had never eaten it before and within about ten minutes of consuming it he had started to react.'

'A lucky young man to be near our hospital,' observed Charmian.

'Too true,' agreed Richard, 'and the amazing thing is he got over it so quickly. It's an interesting case and John Pickard and I are going to write it up for one of the journals.'

'Is that why you are doing further investigations?' asked Charmian, interested.

'Yes, we might as well while he is in the area,' replied Richard. 'Which reminds me the ballet company are going to give a charity performance in two weeks' time and I think the Unit will be lucky enough to benefit. We should be able to acquire money for two or maybe even three respiratory monitoring systems.'

Richard's face lit up with enthusiasm as it always did when he talked about his beloved Intensive Care Unit. Charmian found herself smiling back easily. His enthusiasm was infectious.

'You will have to explain to me just what a respiratory monitoring system will do,' she said. 'I've not worked with one before.'

'That's because it is so new,' said Richard quickly, and proceeded to launch into complicated detail.

'So you see,' he finished, 'if we monitor respiratory signs, then changes in resistance, compliance, end tidal CO_2 and tidal volume would immediately indicate changes in pulmonary status and could assist in the early diagnosis of such conditions as pulmonary emboli and bronchospasms.'

Charmian made a mental note to go to the library and read the latest literature available on the subject as soon as possible. If such a piece of machinery was going to be installed she had better make sure she was able to understand what it could do. Richard, as usual, had rattled off so many facts and figures that he had left her feeling quite dazed.

By now he was sitting back even more comfortably with his second cup of coffee and looking as if he was esconced for the evening. Charmian put down her coffee-cup on the tray, wondering what she should do to make him move. Oh well, she thought resignedly, there's nothing for it but to ask him to go. She stood up.

'Thank you, Richard, for bringing me home but now I'm going to have to throw you out, I'm afraid—I have quite a few things I must do. I *did* tell you.'

Was it her imagination or did genuine regret flicker across his face? He put down his cup slowly and fixed her with a searching gaze.

'What are all these important things that you've got to do?' he asked.

'Really, Richard, I don't think I have to explain anything to you,' returned Charmian, agitated.

'Oh yes you do,' said Richard, standing up and towering over her, 'you have to explain what, or *who*, is so much more inviting than having dinner with me.'

Charmian began to see red at his presumption. Forgetting their easy companionship of a few moments before, she flashed back angrily at him for presuming too much.

'Outside the unit my private life is my own,' she heard her voice saying,' and *I* choose with *whom* I am going to spend my time and *how* I spend my time—and I choose *not* to spend it with you!'

Walking over to the door she flung it open. 'Goodbye,' she said pointedly.

He held her gaze for a fraction of a second, his eyes dark and angry as he strode forward. His hard glance lashed over her as he brushed past her in the doorway. Charmian involuntarily recoiled. There had been a look in his eyes, almost a promise, that said he wasn't giving up, only postponing the inevitable.

Once outside the door he turned and putting his hand on the jamb to prevent her from closing it, looked at her long and hard. It seemed to Charmian that they stood there like that, their eyes locked in silent combat, for a lifetime, although in reality it was only a split second. Richard seemed about to say something but then changed his mind and, swinging on his heel, left abruptly.

Sighing deeply Charmian closed the heavy door. There seemed no way in which she and Richard could spend very long in each other's company before they were quarrelling. And what did they quarrel about? It was always the same thing that triggered it off—he was too domineering and she was too defensive.

If only we had never kissed, she thought—*then* perhaps I wouldn't be so on edge. But she knew really that it wouldn't have made that much difference, she had been on edge ever since she had first set eyes on him. He had stirred deep, smouldering fires within her that were difficult to quench.

She cleared up the coffee things with a heavy heart, not looking forward to the rest of the evening at all. All those fictional interesting things she had to do so urgently! Reading a book, writing letters and washing her hair! What an exciting prospect for the evening . . .

As she put the last coffee cup away the telephone rang.

'Hello, Charmian Williams speaking,' she answered.

'Good evening,' said a familiar voice. 'Is that Sister Williams from the Intensive Care Unit?'

'Yes it is,' replied Charmian, 'that's Anton Kiminski, isn't it?'

'Yes, are you surprised?'

Charmian laughed. 'Yes and no. Nothing would surprise me where you are concerned.' Then she remembered the roses. 'Thank you for the roses, they were a lovely surprise and they are simply beautiful.'

'I'm glad you like them,' replied Anton. 'It is my way of saying sorry. Now to get down to business, can you have dinner with me and some of my friends tonight? We are not dancing and there is a very good Italian restaurant, La Porta Rosa, near the theatre.'

She hesitated, unsure—the invitation was tempting.

'Come on,' his voice was persuasive. 'We won't be

staying late because there is rehearsal tomorrow for everyone except me. I'm still officially sick!'

Charmian made up her mind quickly. 'Yes, that would be lovely,' she replied.

After they had made arrangements to meet outside the restaurant Charmian replaced the receiver on its cradle slowly. She wondered whether or not she had done the right thing. But then, she told herself, why not? She shouldn't always be so cautious, what was the matter with her? Her life wasn't terribly exciting and she had never been asked out to dinner by someone of international repute before. Nor ever likely to be again, she reflected wryly. So she made up her mind to grasp the opportunity with both hands and enjoy herself.

She showered and changed quickly, slipping on a pair of bright green baggy pants which fastened at the ankles with green laces. With it she teamed a loose silky blouse in a paler shade of green, cinching them together with a wide belt. It was quite an adventurous outfit for her and one which she had not worn since coming down from London because it had seemed too fashionable. But theatrical people, she reasoned, were sure to wear the last minute in fashion, so she wouldn't stick out like a sore thumb!

She met Anton outside the restaurant as arranged.

'Charmian, my dear,' he kissed her hand. 'You look even more ravishing out of uniform.'

'You certainly do my morale a power of of good,' she laughed, as he escorted her into the restaurant.

The crowd of people he introduced her to were all very friendly and the restaurant had an exuberant Italian atmosphere. Charmian began to enjoy herself in a way she would not have thought possible at the beginning of the evening. Food just kept arriving, plate after plate.

Charmian had no idea who was ordering, for the meal had the easy conviviality of a huge family gathering. She tried all kinds of dishes she had never tasted before. First she had antipasti, then pasta with mussels. In spite of being a dancer and presumably having to watch his weight, Anton was passionate about food and he was anxious that she should try everything. The main dish was a delicious duck platter called Anitra alla Venezia.

'I must get an Italian cookbook,' Charmian exclaimed as she tasted the mouthwatering dish, 'and try this recipe myself.'

'Then you must promise to ask me to dinner some-time,' rejoined Anton.

'When you come to this part of the world again I will,' promised Charmian, thinking, however, that it was extremely unlikely.

The rest of the evening flew by. Charmian was in-cluded in the conversation which ebbed and flowed around a diversity of topics. Anton told everyone about his bad behaviour in the hospital and how he had put poor Charmian in a compromising position!

'I must say you don't sound in the least bit sorry!' Charmian couldn't help laughing at his description of the events. 'But anyway, you have said sorry in the nicest possible way, by sending me roses and asking me out to dinner. It's been a lovely evening.

'So he *should* do something to make up for it,' said one of the girls. 'I don't know why you didn't hit him. Behaving like that when he was supposed to be a patient!'

'Well he was a patient and you just don't hit patients, especially not those in the Intensive Care Unit! and anyway,' she smiled, 'it wasn't really as bad as he has made out.'

The meal finished with coffee and grappa all round, a new experience for Charmian. She found the grappa fiery but softer to the palate than whisky. At last it was time for goodbyes and she took her leave of the company,

'See you at the charity performance,' they chorused as she left with Anton.

'Oh yes, Dr West said something about that,' she remarked as they walked back to her car. 'Had you planned to do this all along?'

He put an arm round her in easy familiarity as they walked along. Charmian didn't object, she knew he was very attracted to her but she also knew that it was a case of 'here today and gone tomorrow', and anyway the fact that his arm was around her didn't make her legs turn to jelly. Not the way Richard West's proximity always did!

Anton answered her question. 'Yes we had always intended to do this charity performance but we hadn't decided which charities we would donate to. So I suggested that one of them should be the Intensive Care Unit. After my stay there it seemed appropriate.'

'It will be very much appreciated,' Charmian assured him, 'and put to good use.'

'You *will* come to the performance won't you?' he asked.

'If I'm not on duty, I promise,' said Charmian.

They didn't hurry but strolled along looking in the shop windows. Charmian felt relaxed and happy, probably the result of all that food and wine, she reflected! They started to cross the road when a large car coming along on the opposite side drew to a halt.

'Mr Kiminski, I can see you have completely recovered,' came a deep familiar voice.

Charmian's heart thudded against her ribs. Damn Richard West, couldn't she go anywhere without him turning up?

Anton of course, had no reason for not wanting to see Richard West. He didn't mind in the slightest, why should he? He went across to the car, now pulled in at the kerbside, with a very reluctant Charmian slowly following in his footsteps.

'Hi, Dr West. You should have been with us!' He leaned unself-consciously on Richard's open window. 'Charmian and I have just had the most marvellous Italian meal.'

'I didn't know you liked Italian food, Charmian.' It seemed to her that his voice was cold and distant, or was it her overactive imagination?'

'Yes, thank you, I like it very much,' she answered. Then, turning to Anton, she said, 'Look we have nearly reached my car. I'll go now while you stay and chat if you want. I really ought to be going and it's getting late.'

'I wouldn't dream of keeping you two apart.' There was no mistaking the ironic tone in Richard's voice now.

Charmian sighed. It seemed whatever she did got misconstrued by Richard. Although she knew, in this instance, she couldn't really blame him. After all, she had by omission rather than by definition, implied that she had something exciting to do that evening!

Anton moved away from the car window and slipped an arm round Charmian, a fact which she could see was closely observed by Richard.

'Goodbye then,' he said and started leading Charmian away. 'I'll see you next week with the director of the company, when we make the final arrangements for the charity gala.'

'Yes, I'll see you then,' answered Richard, 'and don't keep Charmian out too late, she is on duty early tomorrow morning.'

'What a nerve that man has got!' exploded Charmian as Richard drove off. '*Don't keep Charmian out too late* indeed! Anyone would think I'm a child!'

Anton smiled at her, 'Charmian, don't get so upset. He is very fond of you.'

Charmian stared at him. 'Fond of me?' she questioned . . . 'Whatever makes you say a strange thing like that?'

'Because of the way he looks at you,' replied Anton. 'I can tell these things.'

Charmian snorted derisively, 'I'm afraid you don't know anything, Anton, you are far too romantic.'

'If you don't believe me, why don't you lead him on a little and find out?' teased Anton.

'Because I have far too much good sense. Ours is a strictly working relationship. He is the doctor and I'm the nurse. He gives the orders and I carry them out, and that's the end to it.'

Anton sighed in mock reproof. 'Give him a chance, Charmian. You have no faith in your fellow men.'

'Not in that particular man, I don't,' replied Charmian. Before long they found themselves approaching her little Mini. Anton chivalrously unlocked the door for her and gently kissed her goodnight.

'Remember what I said about Dr West,' he said. 'Give him a chance.'

'Yes, I'll remember,' Charmian replied softly, 'but I'm afraid you are wrong. He doesn't like me for the right reasons—that is if he likes me at all!'

As she drove home she meditated on Anton's words over and over again, and then finally dismissed them. Anton was an emotional, romantic man, not ruthlessly efficient like Richard West, whose only aim in life was to get what he wanted.

As she settled down eventually for sleep that night, a smile of satisfaction curved her lips. It had, on the whole, been a lovely evening after all—and what did it matter if Richard had seen her out with Anton? It was much better than washing my hair she thought sleepily.

CHAPTER EIGHT

IT ALWAYS seemed to Charmian that when a morning got off to a bad start in the unit usually the whole day was disastrous. There never seemed to be any half measures and when she set foot in the unit the morning after her evening out with Anton, Charmian knew it was going to be one of those days.

'Cardiac arrest, number three bay,' shouted Jane, simultaneously pressing the cardiac arrest alarm. She should have been gone as she had been on duty the previous night but she'd stayed on for half an hour as the unit was so busy.

Amid the ordered chaos that follows such an alarm, Charmian was aware of Richard West at her side. In the absence of the technician he helped her push the cardiac resuscitation trolley to the bedside, then he quickly and deftly intubated the patient and instituted cardiac massage and defibrillation. The arrest team worked silently and urgently, responding to the instructions barked out by Richard. After what seemed an interminably long time the ECG oscilloscope sprang into life with a regular blip and the team visibly relaxed.

'You can go now, Charmian,' said Richard. 'Bill will draw up the drugs I want. I'm afraid there is more than enough work for you on the rest of the unit.' He smiled briefly at her and Charmian could see that his mind was already racing ahead, deciding the future treatment of his patient.

Charmian called the nurses to her desk and quickly

briefed them on their immediate tasks. There was a lot to do in a short space of time if they were to get their results back from pathology by the afternoon.

It wasn't until well into the afternoon that the unit was functioning in its usual quiet, efficient way, the way that Charmian felt happy with. It was only then that she felt she could leave and go to the rest-room for a coffee and biscuit.

Once inside the rest-room, she kicked off her shoes and settled herself in a comfortable old armchair, stretching her slender frame luxuriously.

'Bliss,' she said to the other girls, 'I'm so tired.'

'Been burning the candle at both ends?' laughed one of the girls as they started to leave, their brief rest period over.

'I think one of us ought to stay with Charmian,' said another, 'to stop her from falling asleep.'

'Don't worry about that,' Richard's voice cut in coolly across the room, 'I have several things I wish to discuss with Charmian. I think she'll stay awake.'

The girls laughed. 'Tough luck being a sister,' they said, 'no off duty for you!'

Charmian struggled to a sitting position, silently cursing Richard for disturbing her, and hastily took her feet off the chair on which she'd been resting them.

'Don't let me disturb you,' said Richard sarcastically, 'you probably need to catch up on your beauty sleep.'

'You've disturbed me anyway,' said Charmian. 'And that's hardly a fair comment, this is the first moment I've stopped since I came on duty this morning.'

'After a very late night.' Richard's lips curled disdainfully.

Silently Charmian seethed, but she gritted her teeth,

determined that Richard wasn't going to get a rise out of her this time.

'Well?' asked Richard.

'Well what?' said Charmian, purposefully misunderstanding him and opening her deep, ultramarine blue eyes wide in an expression of bewildered innocence that she could see annoyed him.

'Well, did you have a late night?' snapped Richard.

Charmian began to enjoy herself. For once she felt she had the upper hand if only she could keep her cool. Deliberately she slipped her shoes back on and drained her coffee-cup.

'If you are concerned about my welfare, please rest assured that I had sufficient sleep and that I had a very pleasant night!' she said sedately, and slipped out of the rest-room door, leaving Richard sitting there. She glimpsed his face as she left, black as thunder!

Scuppered you, Richard West, she thought defiantly, although her pleasure at having the upper hand for once was dimmed by the knowledge that almost certainly he'd jump to the wrong conclusions.

Charmian went back to her desk and tried to get immersed in her paper work, although the information on the papers in front of her kept going out of focus, only to be replaced by an image of Richard West's darkly haunting face. Out of the corner of her eye she saw him go into his office. Later Carol Miller joined him and then they both left the unit, Carol shouting to Charmian as they walked out, 'I've got my bleep if you need me.'

Charmian nodded and returned to her paperwork, studiously avoiding meeting Richard's eyes.

Try as she might she couldn't concentrate. More and more she wished that Richard could know that she hadn't been planning an evening out with Anton the

night before, and that he, Anton, meant nothing to her.
You are being very stupid, she argued back at herself.
You refused Richard's invitation and made a feeble
excuse. Yes, but that was because I didn't want to get
involved with a philandering womaniser—and it was just
coincidence that my excuse eventually materialised into
fact, she argued.

Her conflicting thoughts chased round and round in
confusion in her head. Charmian sighed and laid her pen
down wearily as Liz came in.

'My word!' she exclaimed, 'Surely things can't be that
bad?'

Charmian heaved a mammoth sigh. 'Oh, I don't
know.'

'You don't know what?' Liz asked curiously. 'Is something the matter, Charmian?'

For a fleeting moment she was tempted to confide in
Liz. To tell her about the tumultuous tide of feelings
Richard aroused in her. To tell her about her doubts
concerning his character and perhaps more than that,
her doubts about herself. But the moment passed
quickly and she said nothing. She was afraid Liz would
laugh at her and tell her not to be silly, so she said
instead, 'I don't know why I'm so tired.' She smiled at
Liz, 'It must be old age creeping on.'

Liz laughed and shooed her away. 'Now off you go,
and get an early night tonight. The trouble with you
young people is that you all burn the candle at both ends
and then wonder why you can't keep up the pace!'

'I'll have an early night, I promise,' said Charmian
collecting her belongings from the drawer. 'Bye, Liz, see
you in the morning.'

Sleep evaded her that night. She tossed and turned,
dozing only fitfully throughout the night so that by the

time morning came she felt absolutely exhausted. This is no good, she told herself fiercely for the umpteenth time. Put Richard West out of your mind once and for all!

It was in this fiercely determined frame of mind that she went off to the unit in the morning. But much to her annoyance and frustration she had got herself keyed up for nothing. Richard wasn't there, so she couldn't put her new found determination to ignore him to the test!

Carol informed her that Richard had gone off at a moment's notice to give some lectures at a symposium being held in Amsterdam. He was taking the place of another intensive care specialist who had gone down with flu.

'It *is* a nuisance,' grumbled Carol in a disgruntled voice. 'He may not be able to get back for the charity performance by the ballet company and he'd promised that I should go with him as one of the guests of honour.'

Charmian's heart nosedived into her sensible hospital shoes, although common sense told her that it was unlikely that she would have been invited to the ballet as a guest of honour. After all, she was only a nurse and there were hundreds of those in the hospital. Of course Richard was bound to go with another doctor, and who more likely than the senior registrar?

'It must be disappointing for you,' she agreed smoothly. 'When is the performance taking place?'

'The end of this week,' replied Carol. 'I'm keeping my fingers crossed he will get back in time.'

Charmian said nothing, supposing that Anton had forgotten about his promise that she should see the ballet. Disappointment sharpened her mind and she zipped through her paper work in no time at all,

Richard, for the moment at least, having been put summarily into place right at the back of her mind.

Near the end of the day Jane came across to her and plonked a ticket on the desk in front of Charmian.

'You are going to kill me,' she said. 'I should have given it to you several days ago. John Bourne asked me to pass it on to you.'

Charmian picked it up curiously. It was a ticket for *Swan Lake* at the local theatre and attached to it was a scribbled note. *Dear Charmian*, it read, *Richard West asked if I would escort you to the ballet as he has been asked by the hospital management to take another member of the medical staff (I didn't know he was going to take you!) Anyway it's my good luck! Hope you don't mind having to put up with me, Cheers, John.*

Charmian smiled. Of course she didn't mind putting up with John, although she couldn't help wishing that she had received a more personal invitation from Anton. Still, that puts you in your place, my girl, she thought, smiling ruefully. Richard West is taking Carol and is mixing with all the VIPs and you're going as one of the crowd. Serves you right for thinking Anton Kiminski would even remember you. Suddenly she became aware that Jane was prattling on.

'You know, it was really strange,' she said. 'All these tickets came in a big pile and on the top was a hand-written card stating that sister Williams and Dr West were to have these two tickets.'

'Which two tickets?' asked Charmian puzzled.

'The two you are having silly, except that John has got the other one,' said Jane. 'Richard West apparently has got to sit in one of the boxes with Lady Ashburton, she's something to do with the Charities Trust.'

Jane laughed suddenly, 'Do you know, I think

Richard West was quite disappointed when he couldn't sit with you.'

Charmian raised her eyebrows, 'I think you have a hyperactive imagination, Jane.'

'Well, all I know is,' rejoined Jane confidentially, 'he said he didn't want to sit in a box with a lot of stuffy dignitaries. And if you ask me,' she finished, 'I'm not so sure that he was very keen on escorting Carol either, but she made sure he couldn't get out of it.'

'Well,' laughed Charmian, 'nobody *is* asking you, and what is more, they are never going to!' She changed the subject. 'Now tell me, what is this theatre like, is it large?'

Jane was joined by some of the other nurses and they enthused about the theatre. It was, they told her, over fifty years old, all gilt and red plush seats.

'You must go,' they chorused.

'Well, of course I'm going to go,' said Charmian. 'You don't think I'm going to miss an evening like that!'

'And you must wear something positively stunning,' said Jane. 'It's going to be a really swish occasion. Apparently all the money is being donated to three charities and there is a reception with the dancers and other members of the company on stage afterwards.'

'Is the whole audience invited to the reception?' asked Charmian.

'Don't be silly,' giggled Jane excitedly. 'That would be too much of a crush. No it's just the special people like us. We've been invited backstage as we are one of the charity groups. You know some of the money is going towards some fancy equipment for this unit?'

Charmian nodded. 'Yes, I did know. Although I don't know whether Dr West would approve if he heard you calling it "fancy equipment".' She put the ticket in her pocket. 'If it's going to be like you say, I can't possibly miss such a splendid affair.'

When she got home she carefully put the ticket in her evening bag. She hadn't said much to the other girls at the time but she was looking forward to the evening more than she had admitted. She loved Tchaikovsky's haunting music and being a true romantic at heart she loved the tender love-story of the ballet.

Before she turned in for the night she had already decided what she would wear and had got the dress out and hung it up, even though the event was two whole evenings away! It was a full length, black crepe silk dress, with long sleeves and a deep vee cut out at the back.

The next day John popped into the Unit to speak to her. He didn't get the opportunity to see Charmian very often because he had been moved to a cardiothoracic centre at another outlying hospital as part of his training rotation and the hours were very long.

'Can't stop more than a minute,' he said hastily. 'Dr Milward, the boss, is a real stickler for punctuality. But I had to make sure you were OK for the ballet.'

'Yes I'm looking forward to it,' Charmian assured him.

'OK, I'll pick you up at seven,' said John, and with that he was gone.

CHAPTER NINE

CHARMIAN had hoped to get away fairly early the evening of the ballet. In fact, she had been counting on it she had so much to do—but it was not to be. Three admissions late that afternoon kept her working until just before six and she was due to meet John at seven. Oh well, the usual rush, she thought resignedly as she ran down the road from the hospital. That was one of the main problems of working in a hospital—it was very difficult to plan a social life with any degree of certainty.

All her plans for a leisurely bath and shampoo went out of the window as they had so many times before. But Charmian was used to coping with split-second timing and her experience stood her in good stead.

There was only time for a quick shower. She did shampoo her hair but didn't have time to dry it properly so she had no alternative but to plait it into a single pigtail. Putting on the black dress she suddenly realised with annoyance that she hadn't bought herself the strapless bra that she intended to go with it. There was nothing for it but to wear it without a bra.

She stood back and looked at herself in the mirror. The crepe of the dress clung to every curve of her body without being too revealing. It looked very good on her without a bra and her breasts, although small, were round and firm. The whole effect was sophisticatedly sexy and very dramatic, set off to perfection by the shimmering pigtail hanging demurely down her back. But Charmian had no time to really inspect herself, there was only time for a quick glance at her reflection before the door bell rang signalling the arrival of John.

He was dead on time. Charmian picked up her evening bag, checked just to make sure the ticket was still there and flung a silver lamé shawl around her slim shoulders.

John gave a long low whistle of appreciation as she opened the door.

'I hope you've got the hood up tonight,' she said as they hurried down the garden path.

'Don't worry, of course I have,' said John. Although the weather was warm in the day now it was still freezing at night. He looked at her large expanse of bare back. 'I think I'd better have the heater on as well. Do you think you are going to be warm enough?'

Charmian laughed. 'Probably not,' she replied, 'but I'll suffer. I wanted to look glamorous tonight. I didn't want to look like Sister Williams from the Intensive Care Unit.'

'Well, you've certainly managed that transformation all right,' murmured John appreciatively. Then he added, 'I shall be the envy of every man in the theatre tonight!'

'Flattery will get you nowhere,' replied Charmian with mock severity.

'I know,' he answered morosely. 'You needn't remind me.'

The envy of every man in the theatre, John had said. Charmian wondered whether Richard West would be there and if she would see him. She had dressed with him in mind, even though she hadn't admitted it to herself. But even if he hadn't got back from Amsterdam she was going to enjoy the evening—she knew that the moment she entered the theatre foyer.

The theatre was just as the girls had described it. Charmian was amazed at its size. The foyer was an enormous semicircle, brilliantly lit with chandeliers, the light reflecting onto the polished marble floor decorated with intricate art nouveau designs.

Their tickets were in the circle and so they slowly made their way through the crowds and up the great curved staircase which was covered with a sumptuous, thick, red pile carpet. The density of the carpet muffled any sounds their feet made.

Charmian paused for a moment, putting her hand on the gilded balustrade, and looked down on the glittering scene below. She was glad she had worn her black dress. The men and women in the foyer were all wearing evening dress, the women's jewellery shimmered and sparkled in the light of the chandeliers. She wished she had remembered to put some on herself, but it had been such a rush to get out. Anyway, she didn't have anything that could have possibly come up to the quality of the jewellery she saw around her. So on second thoughts perhaps it was just as well!

Turning back from the glittering scene, she raised her eyes and started mounting the stairs again. Her heart lurched uncontrollably in her breast as she saw Richard West standing at the top of the stairs looking down at her with an inscrutable expression on his face. By his side was Carol Miller in an exotic purple and gold dress with a plunging neckline that left little to the imagination.

As John and Charmian came level with them Richard acknowledged their presence with a courteous nod of his head. John said a cheerful good-evening, but Charmian only smiled briefly and endeavoured to get past them as soon as possible without it appearing obvious. She had been hoping that Richard would come and now that he had she was trying to ignore him as usual!

There were still fifteen minutes before curtain up and John suggested a drink in the circle bar.

'There are bound to be quite a few people we know in there,' he said.

He was right, but the bar was so crowded it was like a battlefield so she waited near the doorway while John fought his way to the counter. The hubbub of conversation, the fascinating snatches of gossip that came her way every now and then, gave an atmosphere to the place that she enjoyed. Drinking it all in she idly watched the fluid fingers of smoke from the many cigarettes, curling and twisting towards the ceiling, eventually to merge in a misty blue haze beneath the dimmed lights of the bar.

Charmian was so intent on the scene before her that the sound of Richard West's voice at her side startled her.

'You are the only woman I have seen here devoid of jewellery,' he said in a low voice.

'We were very busy in the unit and so I was late leaving,' she said defensively, turning to him. 'I hardly had time to get ready at all.'

'Don't be so prickly,' Richard replied smiling. 'If you had given me the opportunity to finish what I was going to say you wouldn't have jumped down my throat.'

'Sorry,' murmured Charmian.

'I was going to say,' continued Richard, 'that even so, you are the most strikingly beautiful woman here.'

Charmian felt the pulse in her throat fluttering wildly and knew she was blushing. This was a different Richard West again! He was being gently flattering without being threatening. She lowered her eyes, her thick fringe of dark lashes masking the confusion that reigned within her.

'While we are alone, in a bar with several hundred people,' said Richard ironically, looking around him at the crush and raising his eyebrows, 'I want to apologise to you. I would have preferred a more private place to say this,' he said, looking around again at the crowded bar, 'but to all intents and purposes we are alone at this moment. I want to apologise for my rudeness to you the other night.'

Charmian gazed at him in astonishment as he carrried on. 'You were quite right. Your private life is none of my business and I shouldn't intrude if you don't want me to.'

Charmian averted her agitated gaze to the floor, the long sweep of her lashes fluttered against her high cheekbones.

'I am partly to blame,' she whispered almost inaudibly, 'I encouraged you by my behaviour to believe that . . .' she was searching for the right words with difficulty. 'I encouraged you to think that I was a different sort of woman, different to the person I really am.'

Slowly she raised her brilliant blue eyes to meet his. 'I'm sorry,' she murmured.

'I'm not,' he said looking at her strangely, but before they could continue their conversation any further Carol Miller swooped down upon them.

'There you are! I've been looking everywhere for you in this crowd,' she said slipping her arm possessively through Richard's and giving him a provocative smile.

'Have you got me that drink you promised me yet?' she demanded.

'Sorry,' Richard replied, not sounding at all sorry. 'There's such a terrible crowd at the bar, so I've been chatting to Charmian here.'

Carol's face hardened as she glanced at Charmian, taking in her outfit, hair and makeup in one swift look.

Flashing Richard a brilliant smile she turned in towards him ever so slightly, so that the front of her dress dipped even lower, showing more cleavage than ever.

'I do think it's brave of Charmian to dress so plainly for this evening. Don't you Richard?' she asked. Then turning back to Charmian she said, 'Or didn't you realise, dear, that this was an evening dress affair?'

'Oh yes, I realised,' Charmian replied as coolly as she could manage, even though she was longing to slap Carol's bitchy face. 'This is an evening dress.' And with that she inclined her head graciously to both of them and turned and walked over to John, giving both Richard and Carol the benefit of the view of her satin-skinned back, lithe and supple, with her dress open at the back down to the curve of her buttocks. She couldn't resist giving her hips a sensuous swivel as she walked across to John who was staggering through the crowd precariously clutching the drinks.

John handed her a drink, then took a sip of his own. He looked over her shoulder with a puzzled expression.

'I don't know what had happened over there,' he said, 'but Carol Miller looks as if she had just eaten a sour apple and Richard West is killing himself with laughter.'

Charmian didn't flicker an eyelid. 'I can't think,' she said demurely, sipping her gin and tonic, but a secret smile lurked in the corner of her mouth.

The first bell rang shrilly over the noisy hum of conversation in the bar.

'Oh!' groaned John. 'We shall have to drink up, there'll be a mad rush for the seats now.'

They finished their drinks quickly and John jostled and fought his way back to the bar to deposit their glasses. There was more hubbub than ever now, everyone examining their tickets to see which side of the circle to enter. Charmian looked vainly around for Jane or any of the other girls from the unit but couldn't see them. She had no idea where their own seats were as she had never been to this particular theatre. She just hoped they would have a good view.

She loved the ending of *Swan Lake* and could always remember her disappointment as a little girl when she couldn't see the silver swan gliding across the stage at the end of the performance because her Aunt had got tickets too far on the side. John came back hurriedly and she gave him her ticket and he looked at the numbers.

'The centre aisle I think,' he said and went across to one of the usherettes who nodded and showed them to their seats. The house was full and Charmian settled herself, contentedly listening to the gradually diminishing hum of the audience as they settled in preparation for the performance.

'I wonder who should be sitting next to us,' said John leaning over and looking at the two empty seats next to Charmian.

'Whoever it is they had better hurry or they'll miss the performance,' replied Charmian. 'The houselights are dimming already.'

The auditorium gradually faded into complete darkness, except for the orange glow of the exit signs around the periphery of the theatre. Charmian leaned slightly forward. They had a perfect view. They were sitting almost in the centre and she could clearly see the orchestra in the pit, illuminated by the splashes of light from their music stands.

The musicians were tuning their instruments and waiting for the musical director to appear. The lime from the back of the circle suddenly shone down into the pit and the musical director came up through the small doorway in the centre and, mounting his rostrum, faced the audience to take his bow.

During the applause Charmian was conscious of two people, a man and a woman, squeezing their way past the people at the other end of the row and making their way to the vacant seats next to her. Thank goodness they chose to go that way and not come past us, thought Charmian, and then promptly forgot about them as the orchestra started to play the overture.

It was a large orchestra, at least seventy instruments, and the accoustics in the theatre were perfect. The haunting melodies rose up to the high, domed roof, ringing true and clear, gving the music an ethereal, mysterious quality. Charmian leaned back in her seat and closed her eyes. She just wanted to let the music soak into her, she loved it so much.

Then when the overture had finished and the heavy red and gold curtain rose on the first act Charmian sat entranced. The company used the original choreography, which in her opinion could never be improved upon. Knowing it so well, she loved every single minute of it.

When the curtain descended at the end of the first act and the houselights came up she turned to John, her blue eyes shining. 'It was marvellous wasn't it?' she asked.

'Well,' replied John slowly, 'it was all right.'

'All right!' echoed Charmian. 'It was magnificent, and did you notice how well Anton danced. His leaps!' she sighed. 'You would never have thought he was a patient in the unit only a short time ago.'

'Oh yes, Anton Kiminsky,' said John. 'Yes, I've heard all about him! But I must say, I'm still not all that keen on all those blokes leaping about in those awful tight tights!'

Charmian laughed mischievously. 'John,' she teased, 'don't tell me you are one of those men who get embarrassed at the sight of male ballet dancers?'

'Let's just say that if I had a son I wouldn't want him to be a ballet dancer,' replied John.

'Prejudiced, that's what you are,' laughed Charmian as they stood to make their way back to the bar to collect the drinks previously ordered for the interval.

'It's easier if we go that way,' indicated John, pointing to the left. 'There seem to be a few less people there.'

Charmian turned to go in the direction he had pointed and suddenly realised with surprise that it had been Carol Miller and Richard West who had come in late and were sitting on her left. A fact which obviously didn't please Carol much, judging by her expression.

'Hi,' said John over Charmian's shoulder, 'excuse us pushing past but we have drinks to collect.'

'I thought you two were sitting in one of the boxes with the VIPs,' said Charmian.

'We were supposed to be,' rejoined Carol indignantly, 'but Richard very graciously offered our seats to some Mayor or other as the boxes were too crowded and we ended up here.'

'I prefer it here,' said Richard briefly. 'We'll join you for a drink.' He eased his long, lean form from the constriction of the theatre seat. How tall he is, thought Charmian. His height struck her because, surrounded as he was by so many other men, it was obvious that he was a good head and shoulders taller than most of them. His dark gaze ensnared hers in a sensual caress that caught at her throat, upsetting her heartbeat and sending quivers of agitation down her spine. Charmian was oblivious to everyone around her, trapped by his gaze. The spell was broken by Carol's petulant voice.

'I'm not thirsty,' she said reaching up and pulling at Richard's hand.

'Then we'll meet you back here,' he replied, deftly retrieving his hand and extending it to Charmian.

With his burning gaze on her Charmian felt powerless to do anything but to put her hand in his and follow him. Following Richard, her hand clasped in his, Charmian could see the outline of his muscular shoulders rippling under the velvet jacket of his evening suit. An electric current seemed to be passing from their fingertips, one to another. She longed again to run her fingers through his thick dark hair and caress his strong neck. When they reached the bar Charmian shyly withdrew her hand. There were many other staff from the hospital there—it wouldn't do to be standing there hand in hand with the consultant in charge of the Intensive Care Unit!

John caught up with them and they stood there, the three of them. There was a long silence.

'I'll go and get the drinks,' John muttered uncomfortably, his brown eyes looking at Charmian soulfully, like those of a stray dog. Suddenly she realised that her feelings were written plainly all over her face for all to see. Including Richard West!

I've only just managed to extricate myself from one difficult situation with him and now I just walk like a mutton-head straight into another one, thought Charmian. I'm a fool! As soon as this man has got what he wants he'll drop me for another woman. I'm not going to be one of his women, I'm not! Trying to appear as casual as possible she asked him if he enjoyed the performance.

'I enjoyed watching you enjoy it,' he said indolently. 'Your face is very expressive, you know.'

'You were supposed to be watching the stage, not me.' Charmian felt annoyed that he had been observing her when she had been unaware of the fact. There was something almost possessive in the way he was looking at her and his way of speaking.

'I shall watch whatever I choose to watch,' said Richard giving her a devastating smile, 'and I choose to watch whatever entertains me most.'

It was that word entertain that made Charmian's hackles rise. He had chosen the wrong word! *Entertain* indeed. As if she were some plaything. A puppet on a string, to jump whenever he pulled the strings!

She could see the fire of desire in his eyes as they lingered on the curvacious swell of her breasts. She was acutely aware of the points of her nipples straining against the thin, silk crepe of her dress and began to wish she had worn a shapeless sack!

'I didn't come out this evening with the intention of entertaining you,' snapped Charmian, taking a step away and searching vainly in the crowd for a sight of John and a haven away from this man who disturbed her so much. A steel band gripped her wrist, restraining her movement.

'Oh, but you have entertained me, my dear!' The raw sensuality in his low voice sent wave after wave of shivering, icy fire through the pit of her stomach. 'And I've no doubt you will entertain me even more in the future.'

Charmian turned her head so sharply that her pigtail flew round and almost slapped him in the face.

'Let me go,' she hissed angrily, tearing her wrist from Richard's grasp.

At that very moment, luckily, she caught sight of John and without a backward glance at Richard she struggled determinedly through the crowd over to him.

'I thought we were with Richard,' said John, looking slightly puzzled. 'I thought you wanted to be with him,' he added.

'Well you thought wrong,' snapped Charmian sharply. 'He was talking to some other people and I found the whole conversation extremely boring.'

'Oh,' muttered John, curiously watching Charmian's angry expression. 'Anyway, Carol has obviously changed her mind, or couldn't bear being left on her own. She is up here with him now.'

Richard had completely spoiled the rest of the evening for Charmian and she couldn't concentrate on the second half of the performance. She was altogether too conscious of his presence next to her. Somehow he had managed to sit Carol in the seat he had previously occupied so that now he was sitting next to Charmian. He made no effort to speak to her, but she could almost feel the air vibrating with the nearness of him. She sat stiffly and uncomfortably in her seat, terrified to even put her arm on the armrest in case she should accidentally brush against him.

At the end of the performance she turned to John.

'I've . . . I've got a bit of a headache,' she lied. 'I don't really feel like going on to the reception on stage. Shall we give it a miss?'

'No we will not,' said John decisively. 'I want to have a close look at those male ballet dancers, especially Anton Kiminski . . . Besides,' he added, 'I rather fancy one of the little cygnets. Second one from the left!'

He looked sharply at her. 'I'll take you home soon though, if your headache doesn't go.'

Charmian was pretty sure John had seen through her make-believe headache and had no alternative but to reluctantly agree to go backstage. She made a mental note to keep an eye on Richard West and to stay well clear of him.

However, she needn't have worried. When they made

their way down from the circle, through the maze of passages to the backstage area, it was obvious that Richard had had to join the other VIPs. He and a few others, including Carol, were with the theatre management and some of the principal dancers including Anton.

John and Charmian were with the rest of the mass of people milling about the stage, all talking at once, laughing and drinking champagne. Enormous trays full of glasses of bubbly were being brought round and as Charmian sipped hers it reminded her of the last time she had tasted champagne, at Richard's house.

Everyone was very friendly. The dancers were enjoying their relaxation after their performance and before she knew it Charmian soon found herself caught up in the animated conversations going on all around her.

Suddenly Anton and one of the other male dancers extricated themselves from the VIPs and made a beeline for Charmian. Anton introduced his friend as Roger and Charmian introduced John. There was no doubt about their masculinity from the way they flirted outrageously with all the girls and Charmian could see John's eyes wide open in surprise. He was no match at all for their quick-witted, extrovert behaviour. Roger also made it obvious that he found Charmian attractive and she soon found herself laughing helplessly.

Then, remembering what John had said about one of the *corps de ballet* and thinking he was being a bit left out, Charmian asked where all the girls were.

'If I'm enjoying myself with you,' she said mischievously to Anton, 'I can't leave my companion out in the cold.' She indicated John. 'Second little cygnet from the left,' she told Anton.

John turned a brilliant red with embarrassment.

'No, no,' he protested.

'Your wish is my command,' said Anton, giving an exaggerated bow and sweeping the stage expansively with his hand, and sure enough he was back in a few minutes with the right girl.

Her name was Nina and she seemed pleased to have been singled out for an introduction and was even more impressed when she found out John was a doctor. Charmian laughed and drank another glass of champagne. The company and the champagne were beginning to go to her head. Anton and Roger were immensely entertaining, telling the most outrageous stories of their escapades on tour. The tricks they played on each other, the awful digs they often had and what their landladies had to put up with!

'You sound as if you are one big family,' said Charmian. She had forgotten about Richard for the moment and was feeling exhilerated and slightly intoxicated. The chatter on stage was stilled by an announcement over the loudspeakers.

'Ladies and gentlemen, pray silence please. We now have the honour and privilege to introduce to you Lady Ashburton, who will present the donations to the chosen charities. Donations made possible by this performance tonight.'

There was a polite ripple of applause and an imposing woman with rigidly set, grey hair stepped forward to the microphone that had been placed centre stage. Charmian didn't know the people who received cheques for two of the charities. One was for a school for mentally handicapped children and the other was for the local youth orchestra.

Then Richard West stepped forward. He looked very distinguished as he gave a little bow and accepted the cheque for equipment for the unit. He obviously charmed Lady Ashburton for she remained deep in animated conversation with him long after the ceremony was over and everyone else had gone back to drinking and talking amongst themselves.

Yes, thought Charmian cynically, age is immaterial. You just charm any woman you meet!

By now Anton had out-manoeuvred Roger easily and had his arm around Charmian's slim waist. She didn't object. She was flattered and pleased that he hadn't forgotten her after all, and anyway, what did it matter if Richard should happen to catch a glimpse of them? She was free to flirt with whoever she liked!

'I have been dying to see you all evening,' said Anton theatrically, his dark eyes laughing.

Charmian wagged her finger at him reprovingly. 'You should really be with the VIPs,' she said.

'Not when I've got the chance of being with you.' He slid his fingers tighter round her waist. She noticed for the first time that his English had quite a pronounced foreign accent and thought perhaps he had had a little too much to drink. By way of diversion she called to John, who seemed very taken with his little cygnet.

'Anton,' she said when John had joined them, 'would you take John and I backstage and show us the lovely swan that glides across at the end of the ballet? I'd love to see it really close to.'

Anton readily agreed. 'Come on,' he said letting go for a moment of Charmian's waist, which had been the whole object of the exercise!

'What did you do that for?' asked John frowning at Charmian. 'I'm getting on very nicely, thank you, as I am.'

'Oh, please, John, *do* come,' pleaded Charmian

under her breath. 'I don't want Anton to get too amorous.' Then she added, 'Bring Nina as well.'

'You can bet on that,' replied John. Nina was evidently doing his ego a power of good. She was very small and Charmian could see that he enjoyed having a girl he could look down on for a change.

They made their way through the throng towards the back of the stage. Charmian found the whole backstage area fascinating and Anton was in his element explaining everything to her. So engrossed was she that she failed to notice that John and Nina were no longer with them when they finally reached the huge model of the swan.

'I think perhaps we'd better go back now,' said Charmian, looking around for a sign of John.

'No! Come on,' said Anton nimbly climbing up. 'Come and sit in it.' He reached down and lifted Charmian up into the swan with his powerful arms and placed her in the little seat between the great silver swan's wings.

'Now,' he said, putting both his arms round Charmian and drawing her close to him, 'now, you are my prisoner, my swan princess.'

He was about to kiss her when suddenly they were illuminated in a blaze of lights. Charmian swallowed desperately and wished she could have disappeared in a puff of smoke for there, standing staring at them, were all the VIPs who had been brought round on a tour of inspection. In the forefront stood Richard West. There was an awkward silence. This is what is known as a pregnant pause, thought Charmian, restraining herself with difficulty from bursting into hysterical laughter.

The silence was broken by Richard's sarcastic voice. 'It seems that we have found not one bird, but three!'

CHAPTER TEN

IF CHARMIAN was disconcerted by the sudden arrival of a crowd of onlookers, not so Anton. He couldn't have cared less—in fact he positively revelled in it.

'You are right,' he shouted, standing up and gesturing dramatically. 'We are three. The magic swan, myself and charming Charmian, on whom I have cast a spell.'

He leaped down to the floor and turned to help Charmian. There was no escape and, much as she would have preferred to have hidden in some dark and remote corner, Charmian saw that Anton was intent on introducing her to the crowd. So with as much dignity as she could muster in the circumstances, she allowed herself to be lifted down.

He made a great show of gallantly escorting her over to the nearest group and turned to Richard West who was, unfortunately for Charmian, the nearest person. His words of greeting were interrupted by Richard.

'I had forgotten how well you and Charmian got on,' he said cuttingly. 'We work together, remember!'

Charmian returned his cold gaze with an equally frigid look and felt her embarrassment slowly turning to anger. He had no cause to look so damned self-righteous! Anton seemed quite impervious to Richard's tone of voice.

'Yes, I did forget. You lucky man,' he said jokingly, moving on with Charmian to another group of people. Fortunately Charmian found the people he introduced her to were mainly from the ballet company and they took the whole incident as a huge joke, teasing her and telling her she had a lucky escape, as Anton was well known for flirting with all the pretty girls. Some of the people she had met when she had gone out to dinner at the Italian restaurant were there.

An older woman, who was apparently the ballet mistress, took Charmian under her wing and reassured her.

'Don't worry too much my dear,' she said, noting Charmian's anxious expression. 'In the theatrical world one is used to high spirits. It's our way of releasing tensions, no one thinks twice about such escapades. Someone is always doing something ridiculous, especially when Anton is around!'

Gradually the crowd drifted back on stage and joined the main group at the reception, which by now was beginning to thin a little as people were gradually leaving. Charmian looked around for John, hoping he hadn't disappeared with Nina leaving her to find her own way home! She thought it very unlikely as he had always been the perfect gentleman, but she couldn't help getting a little worried when she couldn't see him anywhere.

Looking around and becoming increasingly anxious, she suddenly saw Richard West coming towards her.

'If you are looking for John,' he said, 'I've sent him off to take his little ballerina out to dinner.' His eyes gleamed mocking. 'I told him you were otherwise engaged!'

Charmian was so angry she was momentarily at a loss for words. Her mouth opened but nothing came out.

'If you stand like that much longer I shall be forced to start mouth-to-mouth resuscitation,' he remarked in an amused voice.

Charmian found her own. 'You had no right,' she began. 'John was taking *me* home!'

'*I* shall take you home,' he announced arrogantly. 'Unless, of course, you are spending the night with your ballet dancer friend.'

He inclined his head suggestively to one side and smiled, but far from mollifying Charmian it infuriated her. The suggestive jibe flared the anger within her to burning point.

'I shall take a taxi,' she snapped back and moved to step out of his way, only to find her path blocked by his tall frame.

'Don't let's have another scene,' he said in a low angry voice, 'I should have thought the episode with Kiminski was enough for one night!'

Agitated, Charmian knew there was no escape as a group of officials came across to them and Richard shook hands with them, saying the official goodbyes and thank yous. Charmian was forced to shake hands and say all the correct words too, which luckily she found came automatically to her lips although it was becoming increasingly difficult for her to think clearly. She could see Anton on the other side of the stage engrossed with another group of people and smiled brightly, hoping that he would see her and come over. But Richard determinedly steered her across the stage and out by the stage door into the car park.

Charmian wrenched her arm away from him as soon as they were outside, but he immediately put his arm round her shoulders holding her in a gentler but just as firm grasp, pulling her close to him.

'Hadn't you better wait for Carol?', said Charmian breathlessly, desperately playing for time.

'Carol came under her own steam as she was due back

on early duty.' He sounded complacent. 'We have no need to wait for anyone.'

As they walked through the car park away from the theatre into the dark shadows, his arm tightened around her. The silence was almost tangible, a crackling current of turbulence. Against her will Charmian felt a desperate ache to be gathered up in his arms again, to melt against him. To feel the touch of his lips, his hands. Almost involuntarily she turned in towards him.

Richard seemed to hesitate for a second. Then, 'You witch,' he murmured huskily, his mouth moving softly along her jawline down the curve of her swan-like neck into the pulsating hollow of her throat.

A kaleidoscope of whirling emotions engulfed her in a sweet mesh of brilliance. His velvet evening jacket was unbuttoned and instinctively Charmian slid her hand inside against the warm silk of his shirt, feeling the hardness of his muscled chest and the faint prickle of his hair beneath the silk material. He in turn ran both his hands down her bare back, pressing her into him so closely that she could feel his need of her. His mouth traced a sensual path of burning desire slowly up her neck towards her face. Charmian arched her neck in sensual gratification and turned her face eagerly, her lips parted to receive his powerfully invading mouth.

Richard gave a low groan. 'I want you,' he whispered.

His whispered words brought Charmian back to some sense of reality and she struggled to regain control before all her defences were undermined completely. She began to push him away.

'People are coming,' but her words were lost as his mouth came crushing down on hers with a passion that left her breathless. Desperately now, Charmian tried to push his powerful body away and the insistent pressure of her hands finally stopped him in his tracks.

'You are right,' he said wryly, 'people *are* coming.' Turning, he unlocked the car door and opened it for her.

Charmian sat in the luxurious seat, her mind in a turmoil. She knew he wanted her, he didn't have to say so! It was patently obvious, and she also knew that if she went back with him to his home and they were alone she wouldn't say no. She didn't want to say no, her body ached for the fulfilment she knew he would give her, but a nagging voice in those deep recesses of her mind kept repeating the word 'love'. She wanted to love and be loved. She had always promised that when she gave herself to a man it would be for that reason, and that was the one thing that did not exist between her and Richard West . . . *love*. They always seemed to antagonise each other even though their physical attraction was a powerful magnet. Somehow I have to tell him all this, she thought. Somehow I have to make him understand!

He opened the door his side of the car and eased his long, lithe form into the seat beside her. Charmian stole a sideways glance at his profile as he turned the ignition key. It was dark, too dark to see properly but she felt sure he was smiling. She knew she must try to make him understand now, before it was too late, that she was not the easy-going girl he thought she was.

'Please take me straight home.' The words sounded weak and ineffectual in her ears.

He stabbed a swift glance in her direction as he swung the car out of the theatre car park into the road.

'Pardon?' his voice sounded suddenly hard and uncompromising.

'I want to go straight home please,' she repeated.

'Why?' came the steely reply.

'Because . . . I want to,' said Charmian lamely. Somehow the right words of explanation seemed too difficult to find.

'You mean that you prefer to go home to bed alone, rather than go to bed with me.' The words were ominously smooth and she paled at their threatening quality. 'Are you saying that you didn't want me as much as I wanted you just now?'

The words lashed at her like a whip, searing her very soul, making her flesh creep with anguish and latent passion.

'No, I'm not denying it,' she cried, clenching her hands tightly in her lap. 'Sexually you arouse me. Physically you have the ability to excite me and . . . yes, damn you, lose control!'

She turned towards him angrily. 'But I don't want to get involved with you in that way, I want . . .' Her words were drowned in a series of high-pitched, rapid bleeps coming from a receiver on the dashboard. Richard leaned forward quickly and picked up the radiopage bleep from the shelf beneath the dashboard, turning it off.

'We must continue this conversation later,' he growled. 'Meanwhile, I must find a telephone.'

A hundred yards further down the street they saw the glow of a telephone kiosk and, parking the car neatly, Richard leapt out to make his call. His face was grim when he returned.

'It's a rail accident, five miles north of town. I'm going straight to the hospital.'

'Count me for a volunteer,' Charmian said instantly.

'Ever been involved in a major disaster?' he enquired matter-of-factly as they sped towards the hospital.

'No, never,' said Charmian her mind racing ahead to the grim possibilities awaiting them.

As Richard swung the big car into the brightly lit bay in front of the casualty entrance of the hospital Charmian could already see some of the accident site team, dressed in their bright orange protective clothing with their identity tabards strapped to their backs.

As she stepped from the car a nurse from Casualty came running forward. 'In here,' she said, leading Charmian into a small room off the main casualty area where clothing was already laid out. An orange boiler suit in flame resistant material, a protective helmet and a tabard with the words *Emergency Nurse* printed on it.

'What size shoes?' said the nurse, as she helped Charmian out of her evening dress and into the suit.

'Size six,' replied Charmian kicking her own high heels off. The girl turned to the cupboard and grabbed a pair of boots marked six. Charmian slipped her feet into them.

'Here, take these.' The nurse pushed a pair of thick knitted socks into Charmian's hands as she ran towards the ambulance. 'Put them on as you are going, you'll need them. It's cold out there tonight.'

Charmian grabbed them thankfully and kept on running. The ambulance was already pulling away slowly and willing hands reached down and helped haul her up inside. Once sure all his crew were aboard the driver gathered speed along the inner hospital road, the blue light on the roof flashing. As soon as they reached the hospital perimeter the siren started wailing out its thin bleak message into the hostile darkness of the night.

Charmian looked at the other occupants of the ambulance. There was a junior anaesthetist, a junior surgeon, two ambulance men and herself. Richard West was sitting in the front talking by radio to the police who were already at the scene of the accident.

The glass partition between the driver's compartment and the main body of the ambulance was pushed back and Richard stuck his head through, his dark face serious.

'Sounds pretty bad,' he reported. 'Apparently the accident has happened in a deep cutting so there is nothing for it but to park everything at the top and climb down and organise the evacuation of casualties.'

He passed some bright orange cards through the hatch. 'Here are your action cards,' he said succinctly. 'Just follow the framework of instructions to start with, we shall obviously need to reassess our course of action depending on the situation.' He looked briefly at the occupants of the ambulance and smiled encouragingly.

'There's a hard night's work ahead of you.' Then he closed the partition and the ambulance surged onwards.

Even at this moment of fear and apprehension at what might await them, Charmian felt her heart leap at the sight of Richard. He had changed in a moment from being the suave, debonair man in evening dress to a formidable creature in workmanlike overalls. His very presence inspired confidence. Charmian was glad he was in command of the operation. She knew they would all acquit themselves well. They had to, simply because he expected it.

She took one of the cards passed to her. The directions were very brief and to the point. They were not to attempt to help any casualties before they had reported to the police and they were to assess the priorities before beginning any rescue or resuscitation work.

'Seems a bit hard not to start helping the first person

you see,' said the young surgeon reading through his card, 'but I suppose Dr West knows best.'

'Ah, that's because there may be someone needing your help more urgently than the first person you see,' said one of the ambulance men, 'Our first job is to get the casualties in order of priority as far as possible and then help those needing the most immediate treatment first.'

'That's something I wouldn't have thought of,' said Charmian. 'Have you ever been on anything like this before?' she asked the ambulance man.

'Yes, just once,' the man replied, 'but this sounds as if it could be a lot worse.'

The ambulance screeched to a halt at the side of the road by a hedge through which an opening had already been made. Charmian could see the steepness of the railway cutting as she climbed from the back of the ambulance. The whole scene was lit up by arc lamps, giving an eerie blueish light that reflected off the twisted, splintered coaches and the great, jagged pieces of metal that were splayed in all directions.

For a split second panic gripped Charmian. Then her professional training rose to the surface and with the rest of the team she followed Richard West stumbling and sliding down the steep, slippery slope to the mass of jumbled wreckage below. When they reached the bottom and arrived at the actual scene the disaster was even worse than it appeared from the distance. The cries of the wounded came from all sides and somewhere down the track a high pitched voice was screaming pitifully for help. At first it was hard to ignore the cries and listen to instructions, but once they actually started on the task of clambering through the wreckage and assessing the priorities Charmian found that she needed all her concentration on the job in hand.

She heard Richard's voice in the background asking for another mobile medical team to be sent out.

'Thank God for that,' said the young anaesthetist with her. 'We'll never be able to manage on our own.' Charmian noticed his face was white with fear and she gave his hand a reassuring squeeze, even though she could have done with some reassurance herself.

Charmian worked with the others throughout the rest of the night. The ambulance men moved the patients who could be fairly easily extracted from the wreckage and the medical team did what they could to those who were injured and trapped. Charmian put up drips, gave oxygen and administered analgesics to those in severe pain and it was only when they seemed to have dealt with most of those still living that she realised that the sun had risen. The arc lamps had been switched off. It was broad daylight. Wearily she helped two ambulance men and a fireman manoeuvre a small boy from under a pile of seats that were crushing his little limbs. He was conscious and in a lot of pain. His small, pale face stood out in the murky grimness of the crumpled carriage and Charmian winced as they had to tug him through the wreckage, but there was no other way. At last they got him out of the coach and then the men began the difficult task of carrying him up the steep embankment.

Charmian leaned against the side of a mass of mangled wreckage, unaware that she was covered in blood, soot and grease. She had lost her protective helmet long ago and her hair was caked in blood. John Bourne came along.

'God, you look awful,' he said. 'How long have you been here?'

'Since the start. I came with Richard West's team.'

Suddenly her legs began to turn to jelly and she slumped, exhausted, in a heap to the ground.

'Do you think we've nearly finished?' she asked John, cradling her head in her hands.

'Well, I think you've finished,' he replied. 'Anyway, we're just waiting for Richard to give the all-clear. The rest of the poor devils,' he indicated the bodies remaining in the coaches, 'are all dead. Nothing we can do for them.'

He sat down beside her. 'You look all in. I didn't even know you were here.'

Charmian raised her head and gave him a tired smile. 'I didn't know you were here either, there wasn't much time for social chatting.'

'I came with the second team,' he told her. He jumped up. 'Here's Richard, looks like something's up.'

Charmian looked up too. Richard West was running along the track, leaping in even strides from one sleeper to another. Although his usually tanned face was drained of colour, he seemed to have as much energy as usual.

'We've just found another survivor, a woman trapped down there,' he waved towards the last carriage down the track. 'She's conscious and in a lot of pain. We are going to have to amputate her arm, I'm afraid, before we can move her.'

He looked at Charmian. 'Are you OK?' he asked brusquely.

She nodded and got up. 'Yes, of course I'm OK. Just tell me what you want me to do,' she said firmly.

He looked at her tired face for a moment, then said quietly, 'Go down with the ambulance man, he will show you where she is. Give her oxygen and this analgesic intravenously.' He handed her a box with a syringe and an ampoule in it. 'We'll join you with the surgeon in about four minutes.'

Charmian took the box from him and ran, following the ambulance man down the rutted track. She surprised herself. She didn't know she had any reserves of energy left.

When she arrived where the woman was trapped, Charmian found her almost hysterical.

'Don't worry,' she comforted in a gentle, calm voice, 'help is here now. Here, hold on to my hand tight and then take some deep breaths of this oxygen.'

The woman grasped her hand desperately, her eyes wide and fearful. 'Help me, help me,' she whispered, her breath coming in short painful gasps, 'please, don't let me die!'

'I'm not going to let you die, I promise you that,' said Charmian, smiling at her encouragingly, masking the fear she felt as she saw the terrible way the woman's arm was half severed through by a piece of jagged metal. Miraculously the main artery was still intact or she would have bled to death within minutes. 'Now trust me, and breathe deeply . . . yes, yes, that's it,' she encouraged her as the woman began gulping in the oxygen.

Firmly Charmian held the mask on her face, encouraging her to breath more slowly and take deeper breaths. Then she slipped the needle of the syringe containing the analgesic into her free arm and had just got her settled when Richard, John and the surgeon arrived. It was necessary to amputate the arm from just above the elbow. Charmian assisted automatically now. She felt as if she were on autopilot—she was no longer consciously thinking about what she was doing, she just did it.

At last they finished, got the woman out and put her

on a stretcher. Charmian pinned a label to her dress stating the surgery that had been carried out and the drugs she had received. This was for the benefit of the receiving casualty team back at the hospital.

The senior police officer on the scene came along and spoke to Richard, who in turn came back to the tired silent group standing amongst the debris.

'We can all go home,' he said sombrely. 'Thank you, all of you. You've been bloody marvellous.'

He turned towards the embankment and started to climb it.

Charmian looked up at the steep and now very muddy sides of the railway cutting. She didn't think she had the strength to climb back up, but she knew she just had to find the necessary strength. It seemed easier somehow if she looked at the ground in front of her and not up—that way she didn't see how far she had to climb. She started walking but soon ended up on all fours, scrambling towards the top.

She gritted her teeth, sweat pouring down her face and streaking the grime and was beginning to think she would never make it when her hands grasped the fronds of bracken that fringed the top of the embankment. A pair of strong arms hauled her to her feet.

It was Richard. He held her tenderly. 'Can you make it to the ambulance?' he asked, concerned.

Charmian managed a feeble grin. 'Just about,' she said. 'I think my batteries are run down.'

He smiled briefly, 'I know the feeling.'

He helped her into the ambulance where the rest were already sitting in weary silence. The doors slammed shut and the ambulance started moving.

It wasn't until she was awakened by being shaken suddenly that she realised that she must have dropped off to sleep immediately she sat down.

'Wake up,' she could hear Richard's voice in the distance, 'you're home.'

She opened her eyes to find her head on Richard's shoulder, the doors of the ambulance open and John climbing down the steps. Still half asleep, she clambered down to join him.

'Have you two got your keys?' called Richard.

'Don't worry,' said John. 'The cleaning ladies will be there now, they will let us in.'

After that, Charmian didn't remember anything until she struggled to consciousness about ten hours later that evening, to find herself still in her filthy, bloodstained, once-orange suit, spreadeagled across the bed.

CHAPTER ELEVEN

CHARMIAN sat up slowly and stretched cautiously. She ached in every limb and as she tried to move she realised she was very stiff and sore. Memories of the previous twenty four hours came flooding back into her mind. What an eventful few hours they had been!

Starting off at the ballet, that incident with Richard . . . still unresolved. Then, to cap it all, the horrific train crash. Charmian shuddered at the memory of it. Now it all seemed totally unreal, like some weird, drawn-out, nightmare.

However, as soon as she started to move the aching stiffness of her limbs reminded her that it was only a few short hours ago and that it had been very real indeed. She painfully made her way to the bathroom. Clambering through that wreckage, she hadn't realised how much bodily effort she had been putting in.

Slipping out of the filthy overalls she began running a bath and poured in a lavish amount of scented bath oil. She felt as if she would need about ten baths to wash away the blood and grime that seemed to have penetrated everywhere. Even her hair was difficult to unplait.

Once she had lain soaking in the warm, scented water for a while she began to feel more like her old self and reached for the shower attachment to begin shampooing her hair. As she washed her knotted hair she noticed blood in the water and, putting her hand to her temple, felt a swelling on the right side of her forehead and what felt like a small gash. Her finger tips glistened bright red with fresh blood. Damn, she thought, climbing out of the bath to find a plaster. She paused for a moment to see the extent of the damage in the mirror and to her surprise she saw it was quite a large cut, extending from her hairline down her forehead for about an inch. Now that she had touched her forehead it was bleeding freely and blood was trickling down her face.

Annoyed, she grabbed some tissues and mopped her face. Then, keeping a wedge of clean tissues pressed tightly to her forehead, she began searching through the bathroom cabinet for a plaster large enough to cover the gash. It was with difficulty that she tried to wash her hair as she couldn't stem the bleeding properly. Finally she managed and dried her hair more or less.

When she had finished she glanced at the time again. It was now ten p.m.—she had missed a whole day's duty. She knew, by the number of casualties they had referred back to the hospital from the scene of the incident, that everyone else must have been pretty busy and had probably worked long over their hours. Deciding that although she still felt shattered she must go to the hospital, she put on her uniform. Before she left the flat she checked in the mirror and saw her wan image. The dressing and plaster seemed to have done the trick on her forehead and the bleeding had stopped, but her face was pale, with dark circles round her eyes accentuating the delicate fragility of her bone structure. She let her hair hang loose, something she normally never did at work, but at least that way it covered some of the plaster and made it less obvious.

Walking slowly up the road towards the bright lights of the hospital, she allowed her thoughts to dwell on Richard West. How marvellous he'd been at the accident, so calm, so dependable. If only he could always be like that. She sighed. Things couldn't be left in the air for ever between them. That kiss after the ballet had started something that had to be finished one way or the other. She knew somehow she had to make him understand that she wasn't available for a casual relationship. Even though she knew her actions every time he touched her must have encouraged him to think otherwise.

She sighed again—she seemed to be forever going round and round in circles. It was going to be difficult but she had to keep her self-respect. She knew that if she went to bed with Richard without love she would be sacrificing all the values she had always held dear. Please let me think of a way, she thought wearily.

When she finally reached the Unit it was surprisingly quiet. All but two of the beds were empty and the two patients who were there were not new ones. They were two men with long-standing respiratory problems. Out of force of habit Charmian walked over and picked up their notes, briefly skimming through them to pick up the salient points. Jane saw her and came across.

'Hi,' she said. 'We weren't expecting you in. I hear you had quite an eventful night after the ballet.' She peered at Charmian's face anxiously. 'Goodness, you look simply dreadful!'

Charmian gave a rueful grin. 'Thanks for the compliment, that's just what I need.' She wandered back to her desk and perched on it, swinging a leg. 'Yes, I suppose you could say we had a pretty eventful night. Did you get involved with the workload here?'

'No.' Jane sounded quite put out. 'I missed all the excitement. I just went home to bed. I wasn't on the list to be called out last night, only on the back-up team and apparently they coped very well here without me. As you can see.' She indicated the empty beds.

'All the patients have been moved back to the surgical and medical wards, so they are pretty busy there, but at least it gives us a breather.'

Charmian was walking towards the rest room, intending to have a coffee with the girls on duty, when the door to Richard West's office opened and Richard came out. Charmian was shocked to see how tired and drained he looked. Lines of weariness were etched around his mouth and eyes, the strain of long hours of duty clearly visible. She doubted whether he had been home at all.

'What are you doing here?' his voice was sharp.

'I came to see if I was needed because I thought the other girls might have worked long hours. As I can see you have done,' she added.

'I've been anaesthetising the woman whose arm we amputated.' He sighed dejectedly. 'We wasted our time though, we lost her about an hour ago. She had internal bleeding and the surgeon just couldn't stop it.' He sat down wearily at Charmian's desk, rolling a pencil absentmindedly between his long fingers. 'If only we'd known last night that she had a leaking aneurysm in her belly. I should have examined her more carefully.' He suddenly seemed so vulnerable, so deflated and different from the confident man she had always seen previously.

'You know you shouldn't reproach yourself,' she said firmly. 'She had no indications of internal bleeding at the time. No one else would have done anything different.'

'I suppose you're right,' he said, not sounding very convinced.

'Have you had anything to eat or drink?' she asked gently.

He looked up, a faint smile flickering in his eyes. 'No,' he replied. 'Have you?'

'Well, actually no, but I have had some sleep, which is more than you have.' Charmian turned to go. 'I'm going to get you a coffee and a bun, or whatever I can lay my hands on.'

'Don't bother,' said Richard. 'You know it's hopeless trying to get any food in this hospital if you miss the times the canteen is open.' He threw down the pencil in an irritable fashion. 'And even the snack bar will be closed now.' He stood up, hands deep in the pockets of his white coat. Charmian looked at him anxiously, he looked awful. He caught her glance and gave an exhausted smile.

'Don't worry, I'm going home now,' and taking a hand out of his pocket he wagged an admonishing finger at her. 'You do the same thing, go back and come in on duty tomorrow.'

As he was about to go he stopped. 'About last night,' he said.

Charmian's heart did a somersault, she had not expected the moment of reckoning to come so soon! He stepped slowly towards her until he drew level.

'I would like to tell you,' he said quietly, 'that you did a really magnificent job of work. I was very impressed with your courage and skill.'

'I didn't do anything more than anyone else,' Charmian protested. She suddenly felt self-conscious. 'I just did the best I could in the circumstances.'

Subconsciously she pushed back her hair, some strands having fallen across her face. As she did so she revealed the plaster. Richard's eyes immediately alighted on it.

'What's that?' he asked.

'Oh,' Charmian pulled her hair across to hide it, 'it's nothing. I somehow managed to cut myself last night but it's nothing much, just a scratch.'

'Has anybody looked at it? Have you had it thoroughly cleaned? Have you had a tetanus jab?' He rattled out the questions, not giving her time to reply.

Taking her arm he plonked her down in her own chair by the desk and leaning forward whipped off the plaster. Fresh blood spurted out and trickled down her face.

'What do you mean, *it's nothing*?' he murmured. 'It's a hell of a deep cut, and you are coming down to Casualty with me this moment to have a suture put in it.'

Walking over to the cupboard on the side wall by her desk, he took out a sterile dressing pack and, ripping it open, came back to Charmian. Gently he applied pressure to the wound while he cleaned the surrounding area with an alcohol-impregnated tissue. When he had finished he gently held her chin cupped in his hand.

'You are a very silly young woman,' he said softly, 'and I'm surprised at you. You of all people should know better than to neglect a wound like that.'

He put another clean dressing on it. 'Here, hold this on yourself while we go to Casualty.'

'Look, I'll go to Casualty if you insist,' promised Charmian, 'but you needn't come with me. You're tired, you go home.'

'No, certainly not,' he snapped decisively. 'I'm going to make sure that you have a good suture put in that cut, and I'm not going to have some young senior house officer doing it.'

He propelled her along the corridor towards casualty at a brisk pace, 'You can't afford to have a scar on your forehead,' he said firmly.

Charmian didn't reply, she was having difficulty in

keeping up with his long legs, even though her own were pretty long.

Once they got to Casualty Richard soon had the senior house officer on duty scurrying around and organised a tetanus injection for Charmian. Then he telephoned the consultant on duty and asked him to come in and put in a quick suture.

Charmian protested again. 'You shouldn't have called him in. I'm quite happy for one of the juniors to do it.'

'Well, I'm not,' he replied firmly. 'I told you before, you don't want to end up with a scar on your forehead.'

'I'm bound to collect a few scars in life,' joked Charmian. She suddenly felt more at ease with him for some strange reason.

'Yes,' his face darkened, 'I suppose you are right.' Then he added inexplicably, 'A hidden scar is often more painful than one that shows.' As his dark eyes looked into her azure ones, Charmian knew that once someone, perhaps a woman, had hurt him badly. She didn't know why that thought should suddenly come into her mind but she felt sure of it. Perhaps that was why he didn't take women very seriously and only trifled with them now, she thought.

It was a strangely intimate moment, made even more strange because of their surroundings, the sterile white and blue cubicle of the Casualty Department. For a moment Charmian could see a deeply sensitive man, a gentle man, capable of a true and tender love. She wanted to reach out and touch him reassuringly but was glad she restrained herself, for as quickly as the moment had come it was gone and he veiled his eyes with the familiar mocking glint. But to Charmian he still seemed extra vulnerable with those lines of tiredness so deeply etched in his strained face. She tried again to persuade him to go and leave her but he refused, saying he wanted to see the job done properly.

At last Mr Summers, Casualty Consultant, came scurrying in. Charmian felt embarrassed that he had been called in from home on account of a small cut on her forehead. He had the reputation of being extremely good and Charmian was slightly surprised to find he was an elderly man with a shining, pink, bald head surrounded by a frill of silvery, tufted hair.

'Hmm,' he murmured, inspecting Charmian's wound, 'do you remember how you got this? Where were you at the time?'

'No, I'm afraid not,' Charmian told him. 'I think I must have just grazed my head on one of the jagged pieces of metal. I had to squeeze through some pretty narrow places to get at trapped patients.'

'More than a graze I would say. It most definitely needs some stitches.' He turned to Richard. 'You were quite right in bringing her along, and by the look of you young man,' he peered over the top of his gold half-moon glasses, '*you* could do with some sleep.'

It seemed strange to Charmian's ears to hear someone giving Richard a lecture and calling him 'young man' in such a paternal way. She was so used to Richard being in command and lecturing everyone else. She gave him a sideways glance out of curiosity, to see how he was taking it. He appeared not to mind in the slightest.

'All right, Bob,' he replied meekly. 'I know you're quite right and I'm going home in just a few minutes. Just as soon as you have fixed up my nurse.'

'Oh so you're his nurse,' Bob Summers emphasised the word his.

Charmian could feel herself blushing. 'Dr West means that I am the sister in Intensive Care,' she said quickly.

'Hmm, I think I know what he means,' muttered the consultant, concentrating on her forehead. 'Now I'm just going to put in a little spot of local anaesthetic,' he said getting out a small syringe. 'You'll just feel a small prick.'

Actually Charmian felt considerably more than a small prick—it was a painful, stinging sensation that made her eyes water copiously. She blinked quickly so that the two men wouldn't think she was doing anything so cowardly as shedding a tear.

Once the local anaesthetic was working it took Bob Summers only a couple of minutes to put in some neat sutures and to draw the rest of the skin tightly together with plastic skin.

'There,' he said looking at his handiwork, 'that's done. It will hardly show even while the stitches are *in situ* and once they are out I guarantee you will be as beautiful as ever.'

He pushed the trolley with the instruments and dressings on across to the senior house officer who was watching. 'Get one of the nurses to relay this,' he said as he turned back to Charmian and Richard. 'And now you two,' he said sternly, 'off you go, both of you.' Refusing to listen to Charmian's attempts at thanking him, he hustled them down the long corridor leading from the Casualty Department.

As they were walking, Richard turned to Charmian. 'Your dress and shoes are in the cupboard in the Unit. The ones you were wearing last night at the ballet. You can collect them now if you like and then I'll drop you off home.'

Charmian hesitated, remembering the last time she had ridden in his car. It seemed that Richard was able to read her thoughts.

'Don't worry,' his voice was subdued. 'I'll not going to make another pass at you.' He sighed and pulled a face at her. 'I'm too tired!'

Charmian couldn't help smiling at his expression. 'Well, in that case I'll gratefully accept,' she said.

They collected her dress and shoes, which had been carefully put in a plastic bag by one of the girls, and walked to Richard's sleek blue Jaguar, which was still where they had left it the previous night.

Charmian turned to Richard accusingly. 'Do you mean to tell me that you haven't moved from this hospital since we got back from the accident?' she asked. 'No wonder you look absolutely shattered!'

'I managed to get about an hour's rest,' he replied as he opened the car door for her.

They drove out of the hospital and along the road in silence, but it was a comfortable relaxed silence this time. Not like the other occasions, reflected Charmian.

They reached the house where she lived and Richard stopped the car.

'Thank you for getting my head fixed, it was good of you to go to so much trouble.' She fiddled with the door catch. In the darkness of the car she couldn't see to pull it back properly.

'Here, let me' said Richard leaning across. As he reached for the handle his large hand closed over her small one struggling with the catch. Charmian knew he didn't do it on purpose and that he wasn't being deliberately provocative, but even so the touch of his hand still managed to raise a tumult of emotions in her breast. He made no effort to release her hand but held it gently.

'You are so slender,' he said softly, 'and yet last night you had the strength of a lion. Or perhaps I should say lioness.'

'I was strong because I had to be,' she said simply. 'I suppose we all rise to the occasion when it's really necessary.'

'Yes.' Still holding her hand in his, he raised it to his lips and, turning it over, kissed it gently. There was no raw passion now, but an almost gentle humility as he pressed his lips warmly and tenderly into her palm. It was a simple gesture, but it was the simplicity that made it so touching.

Charmian caught her breath unevenly as her heart thumped in her breast. Richard raised his head slowly and she could see his profile silhouetted against the light of the street lamp.

'I think I have some idea of what you were trying to tell me last night,' he said at last. 'When we were so rudely interrupted by the alarm.' He turned towards her suddenly and, leaning closer, cupped her oval face between his hands.

'I would like to get to know you better,' he said. 'And I don't mean just sexually . . . I mean as a friend.' His voice sounded almost pleadingly anxious. 'That is, if you are willing.'

Charmian could hardly believe her ears. If she was willing! Of course she was willing, but she found this new Richard difficult to understand. Was it really possible that he could suddenly have changed, genuinely changed and was really wanting friendship.

'Why the sudden change of tactics?' she asked suspiciously.

'You can thank Liz for that,' he replied.

'Liz?' queried Charmian. 'What on earth has Liz got to do with it?'

'She has given me a ticking off, a good talking to.' She could sense Richard was grinning in the darkness. 'She told me a few home truths about myself and also about you.'

'About me?' Charmian echoed. 'Liz doesn't know much about me.'

'She has told me enough to make me more interested in you as a person, even more interested than I already was,' said Richard. 'So what do you say? Shall we agree to a peace treaty and start again as friends?'

'I suppose we could try,' said Charmian doubtfully, 'but somehow I can't help thinking that there will still be some fireworks!'

'They add to the spice of life.' Richard leaned forward and briefly brushed her lips with his. 'Goodnight.' Then gently and slowly his lips traced a delicate path from her mouth, following the outline of her nose and forehead until he arrived at the wound on her head. Tenderly he kissed the plaster on her forehead.

'Goodnight,' he whispered again.

Then releasing her, he leaned forward and opened the door for her.

Charmian stood in the road watching the blue car disappear swiftly into the night. He had certainly given her plenty to think about. As usual!

CHAPTER TWELVE

TRY AS she might, Charmian couldn't settle down. She wandered restlessly around her flat. Mentally she backtracked over everything Richard had said and done in the car. Even just the thought of the way he had held her hand, the way he had so tenderly and gently kissed it, the way his lips had brushed hers, made her tingle in the pit of her stomach. She looked, half smiling, at the hand he had kissed, then impulsively pressed it against her cheek, as if to implant the kiss there.

At last she got undressed and into bed, but after lying there for a few moments in the dark she knew it was hopeless. She was never going to get to sleep! Slipping on her cotton houserobe she went into the lounge and switched on the gas fire. She felt she might as well be warm and comfortable, even if it was past midnight now and quite chilly. Pouring herself a large brandy, she drew up a chair close to the fire and stretched herself out in it.

The warmth from the fire and the brandy began to relax her, but she still couldn't get Richard out of her mind. No use worrying about it though, she thought resignedly, wiggling her toes luxuriously in front of the fire. Everything will sort itself out in the long run, one way or the other. Just relax, she told herself.

The telephone rang. Charmian glanced at her watch. Two in the morning! It must be an emergency of some sort. She knew it was an outside call coming through the hospital switchboard because it was one long ring of the bell and not the usual double ring of an internal call. It was Richard West's voice on the line.

'Are you awake?' he asked rather needlessly.

'Well, if I wasn't, I am now,' Charmian smiled as she replied.

'Oh.' Richard sounded surprised, then he said, 'I couldn't sleep and I thought perhaps . . . ' he hesitated, not a usual thing for him, 'that you might be awake as well.'

Charmian smiled happily, he almost sounded apologetic. 'Actually you didn't wake me. I was already awake. In fact I'm sitting here in front of the fire with a large glass of brandy in my hand.'

'Disgusting! I'm sitting here in front of my fire with an even larger scotch in my hand.' Richard's voice sounded amused. 'I can tell you are smiling.'

'How can you tell that?'

'I can tell from the sound of your voice. It has . . . what does it have? It has a smile in it,' he finished.

Charmian laughed. 'What a strange thing to say, a smile in my voice!' She changed the tone of her voice to a mocking sternness. 'But now that you *have* rung me Dr West, I take it that you have something really important to say to me.'

'Yes,' replied Richard, 'I rang to invite you out to dinner with me tonight.'

'Tonight!' exclaimed Charmian. 'Do you mean now? But it's two in the morning!'

'No, I don't mean this minute, I mean tonight . . . later on today,' he added by way of explanation.

Charmian suddenly realised that they were well into another day. 'How silly of me, but I'm feeling a little disorientated, so much has happened in the last few hours.'

'I know the feeling,' agreed Richard, 'but will you come? You haven't said yes yet.'

'Yes,' she said simply, 'I would love to come.'

'Good, wear that black dress you wore to the ballet, you look fantastic in that, I'll pick you up at eight.' Richard's voice sounded suddenly very tired and he gave a loud yawn over the phone. 'Having got that settled I think I shall now go to sleep.' His voice softened, 'Till eight then, goodnight. Sweet dreams.'

'Till eight then, goodnight,' echoed Charmian softly as she heard the click of Richard's receiver being replaced. Slowly she replaced her own, a gentle smile curving her lips as Richard's words went ringing through her head.

Still smiling, she drained the dregs of her brandy, turned off the fire and, climbing into bed, immediately fell into a deep and dreamless sleep.

It was too much to hope that the unit would stay quiet and of course the next day it was frantically busy. There were five new admissions. Two of them were bad road traffic accidents, so as well as having all the medical problems to help sort out there was the additional problem of distraught relatives being brought in by the police.

Charmian steeled herself to being cruel to be kind, and gently but firmly steered the weeping relatives out and into the waiting-room, where they would not impede the doctors and nurses busy trying to save the lives of their loved ones.

John was back on duty in the unit that day.

'Thanks,' he called to Charmian as she came back from the waiting-room, having calmed down the relatives.

'I'm hopeless with relations, you're good at that. I'm

better at this,' he indicated the central venous pressure line he was in the process of inserting into a very sick patient.

'Don't mention it,' smiled Charmian. 'I'll get a nurse over to give you a hand immediately. You look as though you could do with another pair of hands.'

'I do,' muttered John, concentrating on the end of the cannula he was trying to introduce into the patient's vein.

Richard didn't come into the unit at all that day. John told her he was attending a debriefing meeting on the major disaster. A post mortem, as he put it.

As well as being busy, it was one of those days composed of a seemingly never-ending catalogue of minor irritations—results not coming back from pathology in time, one of the junior nurses getting blood specimens mixed up before she had labelled them, a ventilator breaking down . . .

Charmian didn't stop properly all day, not even for lunch. She just managed to grab a coffee and a few biscuits in a slight lull.

'No wonder you are so thin,' said Jane as she came back from the canteen, 'you never eat anything!'

'I'm all right,' said Charmian. 'Anyway, the food in the canteen is so disgusting most of the time I'm not really missing much, am I?'

'You're right there,' agreed Jane. 'I had pizza today and I think the base was made of concrete.'

It was gone six before things quietened down. Charmian got herself a strong black coffee in order to try to revive her flagging energy and sat down at her desk in the unit, from which vantage point she could keep a wary eye on all the patients.

John came over with a coffee in his hand and pulled up

a chair beside her. 'Hi,' he said 'it seems ages since I last saw you to actually talk to.'

'Yes, it does,' admitted Charmian. 'But it was only the night before last you know. The night of the train crash.'

'God yes,' mused John, 'and the night of the ballet, too.' He sighed. 'It all seems like a lifetime away.'

They both sipped their coffee in tired silence. Then John said, 'I'm off tonight, fancy coming to the cinema? I don't know what's on, but I don't feel like staying in.'

Charmian was about to reply in the affirmative when she suddenly remembered Richard's invitation to dinner. She wouldn't have believed it possible if someone had told her she would forget about it, but in the rush of the day she had not given the invitation a single moment's thought. She looked at her watch and groaned. It was six thirty and he was picking her up at eight.

'What's the matter?' asked John, seeing her look of dismay as she clattered her cup down and stood up.

'I've just remembered that I've promised to be ready for dinner by eight!'

'Well, you've got an hour and a half,' he said, checking with his watch. 'What are you panicking about.'

'I'm not panicking!' replied Charmian sharply, and then was immediately sorry for snapping poor John's head off. 'Its just that Liz isn't here yet and I've got to hand over to her.'

'Oh yes, she is,' Liz's voice from behind startled her. 'Now off you go and stop fussing. I'm sure John will fill me in on any details I need to know before he goes.' Liz turned to John who nodded.

Charmian was out of the unit before she had time to argue. Not that she wanted to, and she was grateful for Liz's timely intervention—it saved any awkward explanations to John.

By the time she reached her flat she had just a bare hour to get ready. Cursing the fact that she always seemed to be running late, particularly when she was going somewhere special, Charmian literally threw off her uniform, leaving all her clothes in an untidy heap in the corner of the bedroom. Normally she was a very tidy person but tonight she was panicking, as John had noticed! I'll put them away before I go out she thought, if there is time.

Although of necessity there was only time to take a very hasty shower and give her hair a cursory wash, she used her most expensive shampoo and conditioner with matching body lotion and talc. After briskly towelling dry her hair, she liberally splashed a matching perfume on her body. The matching toiletries were French and very expensive. She had treated herself to them once when she had been feeling in a very extravagant mood. It was a subtle, musky perfume and sophisticated. Charmian felt that it went very well with the black dress.

She had just had time to blow dry her hair, slip into the black dress and apply a little make-up, when the door bell rang. A hasty glance in the mirror was all there was time for as usual.

Feeling suddenly apprehensive, she opened the door, wondering at the same time whether or not she ought to invite him in for a drink. The flat wasn't very tidy. As she had been getting ready she had scattered more and more things around and had not bothered to stop and pick up a single item.

Richard's appreciative look when she opened the door to him told her that she needn't have worried about looking in the mirror! And almost as if he knew she had been deliberating whether or not to invite him in he said, 'We won't stop now for a drink because the place we are going to for dinner serves the most marvellous cocktails.'

'I don't need telling twice,' smiled Charmian, picking up her stole which she had placed in readiness. Closing the door behind her she lightly wrapped the stole around her shoulders.

As they walked down the path towards his Jaguar, Richard slipped his hand around the back of her neck and gently pulled out some of the hair that was caught beneath the folds of her wrap. For a few seconds he held the silver strands of her hair in his hand. 'I'm glad you wore it loose,' he said. 'I prefer it that way.'

Charmian didn't reply. Partly because the reason she had worn her hair down was to cover the plaster still on her forehead, and partly because the physical reaction erupting from the touch of his hands was overwhelming her.

The Jaguar purred smoothly and swiftly out of the city towards the forest. Charmian recognised the route as the one she had taken on the bus when she had been exploring, soon after her move from London. It was a lovely evening, and the last rays of the sun slanted through the trees, heavy leafed with the translucent bright green of early summer. In the places where the trees were not so dense there was heather beginning to come into early flower, surrounded by great bushes of broom. The brilliant yellow of the broom blossoms contrasted with the subtle purple hues of the heather.

Charmian had started off feeling rather nervous but was surprised to find how easy it was talking to Richard. As easy as it was to talk to John or to one of the other nurses, except that it was infinitely more interesting. On the subject of running an intensive care unit he had positive and well thought ideas. Some were rather controversial but they all had sound principles to back them up. Charmian had yet to see some of them put into practice and she could imagine that he would meet with resistance from some of his more conservative colleagues. Not that those considerations would worry Richard in the slightest, she knew that!

She also found out that he had very positive ideas on practically everything else. Politics, the arts, family life. She learned a great deal about him and was so absorbed in their conversation that she hadn't noticed that they had turned off the main road and were on the smaller road leading to the little town of Hamblington. It was only when the car slowed down to turn the rather sharp corner that led into the top of the steep High Street that she realised where she was.

'I've been here once before,' she told him. What she didn't tell him was that she had seen him here with his sister's children and that she had mistaken them for his!

'I hope you haven't been to Jelly Roll's,' said Richard turning to her. 'I was counting on surprising you.'

'No, I haven't,' replied Charmian, 'Jelly Roll's! it sounds rather strange.'

'It's different,' said Richard. 'I think you will like it, I hope you will anyway. It belongs to a friend of mine.'

He didn't go right down to the harbour, but turned off halfway down the steep hill into a narrow lane. After parking the car at the back of a rambling old house, he led Charmian towards what looked like the kitchen door. There was no sign or anything saying it was a restaurant, just an old door set at the top of some worn stone steps.

While they were waiting there for Richard's ring to be answered, his hand found the curve of her waist and rested lightly there as if to keep her steady. It had the reverse effect! The warmth of it seemed to burn through the thin material of her dress, making her flesh tingle with an acute awareness of him.

From between her thick fringe of lashes she slid him a glance. The sight of his clean-cut profile, with his chiselled mouth and strong jaw, caused the pulse in her throat to flutter wildly and unevenly. Although she hadn't made it obvious, it seemed he knew she was looking at him for he turned slowly and looked at her, his eyes caressing her in a sensual glance that gave her a sinking feeling in the pit of her stomach.

His hand tightened imperceptibly around her waist, his fingers spreading and stretching warmly along her curves. She shivered as a quiver of desire ran up her spine and demurely lowered her eyes to mask the disturbance she felt.

Fortunately for her, at that moment the door opened and Richard ushered her in. A tall, grey-haired man opened the door, beaming from ear to ear.

'Good evening Richard, old chap,' he boomed. 'About time you came again to my dive.'

'Hello, Clarence.' Richard ushered Charmian into the most extraordinary restaurant she had ever been to. She politely shook Clarence's hand. He was pretty extraordinary looking himself. At the same time she was trying to take everything in.

From the outside it looked like any other old country house—quite ordinary. But once inside it was like stepping into another world. A film set, thought Charmian. It was quite dark, lit only by oil lamps hanging from the dark ceiling. The light from candles reflected on the polished wood of the tables.

It reminded Charmian of the inside of a Mississippi steam boat. Not that she had ever been on one, but she had seen them in films. To set the seal on the atmosphere, a jazz band was on a little balcony up a steep flight of cast iron steps leading from the main part of the restaurant, playing blues-type music.

'You like it?' asked Richard.

'It's fantastic,' answered Charmian. 'From the outside of the building you'd never guess that there was anything like this inside!'

'That's the whole idea,' grinned Richard. 'Clarence has quite an exclusive circle frequenting his "dive" as he calls it. Mind you, we all pay heavily for the privilege!'

He escorted her across to a semicircular bar set at the far end of the room. A few people were sitting on some of the high stools set around it and they acknowledged Richard with cheery waves. Behind the bar was the most comprehensive range of bottles Charmian had ever seen in her life. Every size, shape and colour crowded the shelves.

'Is there any sort of liqueur or wine that is not here?' she asked Richard in amazement.

'If you ask for something Clarence hasn't got, he'll go and get it,' Richard answered. 'He prides himself on always pleasing the customer.'

'I wouldn't dare ask for something he hasn't got, I don't think I could think of anything,' laughed Charmian. 'Anyway there is so much to choose from that it's difficult to decide.'

She put her hand on the tall stool, wondering how on earth she was going to manage to climb up in her clinging long dress.

'Allow me,' said Richard quietly, and putting his hands firmly round her waist lifted her up as if she were as light as a feather and placed her gently on the stool. Instinctively, as he lifted her Charmian grasped his forearms. She could feel the powerful muscles on his forearms rippling beneath the smooth serge of his dark jacket. For a timeless moment they stayed motionless, his hands warm and possessive around her waist. Charmian resisted the wild impulse to slide her hands up his arms to his shoulders. If there hadn't been other people present she would have done, but even Richard couldn't make her behave in quite as abandoned manner as that, she reflected wryly. But she wanted desperately to wrap her arms around his neck and to draw him to her, and she knew from the expression deep in the smouldering darkness of his eyes that he wanted it too.

Clarence came bustling round the other side of the counter. 'Now,' he said, completely breaking the spell. 'What shall I get you to drink?'

Charmian let go of Richard's arms and Richard slowly released her waist. At least, he didn't completely release her, only partially. He took one hand away but left the other there, slipping it deftly beneath the edge of her dress so that his hand was resting daringly, intimately at the base of her spine on her bare skin. The challenging look he gave her out of the corner of his eye almost dared Charmian to object. But she didn't! His hand resting there was giving her the most delicious feeling. She knew once more that she wanted his strong hands to caress her bare skin, to caress and fondle every part of her. She looked at his handsome face as he was talking to Clarence. Oh dear, is it wrong of me to want you so much? she thought.

Her dreaming thoughts were interrupted by Clarence's voice. He was getting out an enormously tall glass as he spoke.

'Now, as it's your first visit here,' he said ceremoniously, 'I shall insist that you have my Singapore Gin Sling. It will go perfectly with your dress.'

'Go with my dress?' queried Charmian in a puzzled voice, wondering what on earth the connection could possibly be.

'Yes, oh yes, my dear. Absolutely!' said Clarence with conviction. 'You see in that dress, I think you look like a character out of a Somerset Maugham story. You know divinely decadent and,' he added, eyeing her up and down with twinkling eyes, 'so sexy!'

All the time he was speaking he was pouring seemingly vast, unmeasured quantities of gin, cherry brandy, lime juice and grenadine into a cocktail shaker, which he then proceeded to shake vigorously.

'Have you noticed she's sexy, Richard?' he asked cheekily. Then without waiting for a reply, 'Yes I dare say you have. You have a good eye for that sort of thing!'

'Clarence, please,' remonstrated Richard looking rather uncomfortable. 'I'm trying to impress the young lady.'

'Then you shouldn't have brought her here, dear,' said Clarence pouring the cocktails into the glass and topping it up with a frothy jet of soda water. For decoration he clipped a little red cocktail parasol onto the side of the glass.

'Now, Richard,' he said when he had finished titivating Charmian's drink to his satisfaction, 'what shall I get you?'

'I'll have a Martini cocktail,' said Richard, 'and not too much vodka, please. Remember, I've got to drive back.'

As Clarence prepared Richard's drink Charmian cautiously sipped her Gin Sling. It was very strong but absolutely delicious.

'Mmm,' she murmured to Clarence, 'I'm glad you chose this for me. I really like it.'

'You be careful,' said Richard. 'It will really go to your

head, it's got a terrific kick to it. I don't want to have to carry you home!'

But the ardent look in his eyes indicated that there was nothing he would like better. Charmian wrinkled her nose cheekily at him, and saluted him with her little red parasol. She was enjoying herself!

It wasn't long before Clarence said their starter was ready if they were and personally showed them to a small, secluded table for two in a dark corner. With the light from the candle on the table flickering on his face, Charmian thought once again how handsome Richard was. Dark and virile, more like a sailor than a doctor. Like someone who spent his life in the open air, rather than a man who spent the greater part of his life in the hot-house environment of an intensive care unit.

The dinner was perfection itself. Clam chowder, barbequed spare ribs and salad. White wine with the chowder and smooth red with the ribs, so that by the time they reached the dessert stage Charmian just had to say no, she couldn't manage to eat or drink another thing.

Clarence, however, wouldn't hear of them leaving without having one of his special Jamaican coffees.

'I really don't think I could eat or drink anything else,' protested Charmian. 'Not even a coffee!'

'You will, given time,' replied Clarence. Then to Richard he said, 'It's such a long time since you were here, come and sit in my private sitting-room so that we can have a quick natter before you go.'

'Yes, let's do that,' agreed Richard. 'You don't mind do you Charmian?'

She shook her head, no she didn't mind. Anything Richard suggested was all right by her in her present frame of mind.

Clarence led the way out of the restaurant into an

oak-paneled room with comfortable, shabby furniture and a glowing fire of chunky logs in the inglenook fireplace. He pushed a settee over in front of the fire.

'Now, you two sit there for ten minutes,' he said. 'I'll go and sort out my customers and then I'll be back with coffee for the three of us.'

To Charmian's surprise Richard did the ungentlemanly thing of sitting down first without offering a seat to her. The next moment his arms reached up, pulling her down into his lap. For a second, just a second she automatically resisted. Then she did what she had been longing to do all evening. She slid her arms around his neck and ran her fingers through his crisp dark hair. She fitted perfectly into the contours of his body and his warm breath fanned her face.

'This is better,' he whispered huskily as his mouth sought out hers with an unerring sense of purpose. Her lips responded warmly to his mobile, searching kiss. Her mouth was buried in his, every intimate part of it belonged to him, she was part of him.

Moving one hand she slipped it inside the confines of his jacket. His silk shirt was like a second skin. Her hands wonderingly explored the muscled power of his torso.

The latent passion he had been witholding flared in his kiss, and Charmian responded with a passion that matched his in intensity. Wild vibrations swept through her, she was intoxicated with the taste, the smell of him.

She felt his hand sliding down until it cupped her breast, gently teasing the nipple with his long fingers through the thin material of her dress, until it became hard and erect with desire.

'You're overdressed,' he muttered thickly. 'I want to kiss every inch of you. I want to see your breasts with your hair streaming over them. I want to kiss the curve of your stomach . . .' He groaned with suppressed desire.

Ecstatic, vibrant emotions swept through her as Richard nuzzled her ear and followed the line of her throat down as far as her dress would allow. With her hands she made a tactile exploration of his face, the hard strength of his jaw, the jutting curve of his cheekbones, the soft thickness of his eyelashes. His arms tightened, cradling her against him so that the breath was crushed from her lungs. Her mouth moved eagerly in response to meet his returning lips and a rising tide of warmth engulfed her. She willingly surrendered to the increasing ardency of his embrace, the blood was pounding in her ears, fiery liquid pulsating through her veins, lulling her senses until she was drowning helplessly in a pool of passion and desire.

The sound of the door opening brought them both back to reality with an uncomfortable bump. It was Clarence coming in with three coffees topped with thick cream.

As they broke away from each other, Charmian was conscious that Richard's breathing was as laboured as her own, his dark eyes were aflame with desire. She hastily scrambled from his lap to a place at his side on the settee, brushing back her dishevelled hair into some sort of order, hoping that her face was not showing too much of a tell-tale flush.

With an effort Richard turned to greet Clarence, who had drawn up a small coffee table in front of the fire and was carefully setting down the glasses containing the Jamaican coffee. As Clarence started chattering, Charmian tried to compose herself and give him all her attention. But she was acutely conscious all the time of the pressure of Richard's taut thighs against her own as they sat close together on the settee.

CHAPTER THIRTEEN

CLARENCE drew up a comfortable armchair beside the settee and passed the coffee to Charmian and Richard.

'Mmm,' he exclaimed after taking a sip, 'I must be getting senile in my old age! I should have told you earlier. Carol rang this afternoon. When she knew you were coming here for a meal tonight Richard, she said she'd pop round with a couple of friends and have a drink.'

He looked at Richard questioningly, suddenly realising he had made a *faux pas*. 'Of course, I didn't know you were bringing a lady with you at the time,' he added apologetically.

Charmian could have burst into tears from sheer anger. The evening had been so perfect and now Carol was coming to spoil it all. She knew the tide of emotion rising within her was not just anger, but anger more than tinged with jealousy.

If Richard felt anything at all he didn't show it. 'Is she coming with anyone I know?' he asked lazily, swinging one long leg over the other.

Clarence seemed greatly relieved that Richard wasn't annoyed. 'She's bringing Jean-Pierre and a friend,' he answered. 'They've just arrived in Hamblington, sailed over from Cherbourg today.'

At that moment the door opened and, without so much as a knock, Carol strode in followed by two young men. Charmian sat miserably on the settee. The intimate atmosphere had gone and the room seemed over-crowded.

From where she stood in the doorway Carol could only see the top of Richard's head over the back of the settee. Charmian was down too low to show.

'Richard, darling,' she called. 'We just had to come and see you. You don't come here often enough now. I've brought Jean-Pierre and Pascal, you remember them don't you?' She leaned over the top of the settee and kissed him with easy familiarity on the top of the head. Simultaneously she caught sight of Charmian.

'Oh, hello,' she said. 'Has Richard brought you out here for a treat? That's nice of him.' The tone of her voice immediately made Charmian feel she was relegated to a lower class. She was made aware that she was not part of the exclusive set that patronised Clarence's 'dive'.

Richard stood up to greet the two Frenchmen, who kissed him enthusiastically on both cheeks in the continental fashion. They obviously all knew each other very well.

Carol took command of the situation and introduced Charmian as 'one of our nurses on the Intensive Care Unit'. Charmian felt her hackles beginning to rise. *One of our nurses*, indeed! The cheek! She wasn't *her* nurse, and she didn't even have the decency to introduce her as the sister! Even though Carol had lost no time in making it obvious that she wasn't pleased by Charmian's presence, there was no need for her to be plain bad mannered!

She stood up and drew herself up as regally as she could. 'I am the sister on Dr West's unit,' she said icily, extending a slender hand to each Frenchman in turn. They for their part obviously approved of her blonde good looks and kissed her hand with Latin fervour.

A waiter brought in some cocktails for Carol and her friends and the whole party sat down again around the fire. Clarence added some more logs and soon the flames were licking up the chimney.

Reluctantly Charmian found that she was sitting between Jean-Pierre and Pascal and that somehow Carol, by dint of clever manoeuvring, had managed to seat herself snugly between Richard and Clarence.

It was with increasing annoyance that Charmian noticed that Carol insisted on talking about people and events that the others were familiar with but not her, so that she was effectively excluded from the conversation. Richard, on the other hand, did his best to carefully steer the conversation back onto more general topics.

It seemed that Carol finally got the message that Richard was determined to include Charmian, for she turned to her with a wide smile.

'Tell me,' she said in an unusually friendly fashion, 'has Clarence let Richard show you over the whole of this gorgeous house yet?'

Mystified, Charmian shook her head. 'No,' she said. She was slightly wary of this new, friendly Carol. 'I've only seen the restaurant and this room.'

'Oh, Richard, you must take her,' insisted Carol, and leaning across to Charmian she said, 'You must make him. You must get him to show you the main bedroom. They say it's haunted with the ghosts of ill-fated lovers who hid there once during the civil war.'

She smiled. Her smile was about as friendly as the expression of a cobra before it strikes, thought Charmian nervously, wondering what Carol had in store for her.

'Clarence lets the room out sometimes to friends,' she

continued, her voice suddenly cold and hard. 'It's very convenient if you want to catch the early morning tide, but don't want to spend a cramped night on board a boat.'

Clarence looked distinctly uncomfortable and said nothing. Charmian stole a quick glimpse at Richard. His face was expressionless. The conversation in the room seemed to die but that didn't stop Carol.

'It has the most marvellous wood panelling and a fantastic view across to the sea.'

She paused for a moment, her words dropping like pebbles into a still pool. Then, slowly and deliberately looking all the while at Richard, she said, 'The view is particularly lovely first thing in the morning, at dawn in the half light. Isn't it, Richard?' She slipped her arm through Richard's in an unmistakably possessive gesture.

Moving her arm quickly away Richard deftly disentangled himself and stood up.

'I think it's time I drove you home, Charmian,' he said.

Charmian stood up ready to leave and turned to give her polite and extremely thankful goodbyes. She couldn't get away from Carol's unwelcome presence soon enough.

Carol lounged back almost insolently on the settee.

'My word, Richard has got you well trained, Charmian. One word from him and you obey! But then I suppose I shouldn't be surprised, he always gets what he wants.'

The last sentence was uttered in words of brittle, shining steel with a sharp edge to them. They were intended to dig deep and hurt and they did just that.

Charmian had always known in her heart of hearts

that Richard and Carol had been, or perhaps still were, lovers. She tried to erase the thought from her mind. After all, what he did was his own affair she told herself. She had no right to feel jealous. But she did . . . oh, she did.

Richard disposed of the formalities with lightning speed and grasping Charmian's elbow walked with her quickly out of the room, through the restaurant and out into the cold night air.

Charmian took a deep breath. The air was fresher outside, away from Carol's hateful insinuations.

As they walked towards his car Richard's grip did not lessen and Charmian snatched an apprehensive sideways glance at his profile. His jaw was set in a hard angry line. Although he hadn't shown it in front of the others, she knew now that he was seething with anger. Why? she wondered. Is it because he really doesn't like Carol now, or is it because he just doesn't want me to know they were lovers?

Common sense was telling her to see and acknowledge him for what he was, a womaniser. But her heart was consistently telling her to ignore all the warning signals and to give herself to this man who could weave such a magic spell over her with one look from his dark eyes.

Not a word was spoken. Richard unlocked the car and opened the large blue doors. They got in, still in silence. He put the key in the ignition and was about to turn it when, suddenly, he slid his arm along the back of the seat and drew Charmian to him. As his arms enfolded her gently she automatically slid hers submissively around his neck and bent his head towards her.

She searched for his lips, taking the initiative, releasing a pent up passion that surprised her. For a few moments they were lost in the joy of each other, fused together in the white heat of the moment.

Then Richard drew back. Cupping her face between his hands he said simply, 'I'm sorry.' He didn't have to say anything more than those simple two words. Charmian knew he was referring to Carol and her innuendos, which suddenly seemed unimportant.

Snuggling her head into his shoulder in a submissive gesture, she reached for his hand and linked her fingers in his, marvelling at their smooth strength.

'It doesn't matter,' she said. 'It's been a lovely evening.'

Richard planted a tender kiss on the tip of her nose and started the engine. As they drove back through the darkness Charmian smiled to herself, blissfully happy with her head on Richard's shoulder. All Carol's remarks were forgotten now. The entire world seemed to consist only of the cosy interior of the car containing Richard and herself. Everything else was unreal.

She didn't demur when he passed the road leading to the hospital and her flat and carried on in the direction of his house. When they eventually crunched up the gravel drive Charmian noticed that a light was shining through the curtained windows of the lounge. The house had a warm, welcoming glow in the dark.

'I left the lounge light on and set some drinks ready before I left,' Richard remarked by way of explanation.

They entered through the kitchen as before and Charmian thought again how clinically clean and neat it was. It had the air of an unused room. It needs a family in here, she thought, to provide a bit of muddle! Hector ambled up to meet them, snuffling curiously.

'Good old boy,' said Richard giving his ears an affectionate pull. He gave him some dry biscuits and fresh water and then shut him in the kitchen.

As they walked through into the lounge, Richard took Charmian's stole from her shoulders and tossed it lightly over the back of one of the chairs.

'Do you want a drink now?' he asked, waving a hand towards a silver tray with glasses on standing on the sideboard.

'No, I don't think so now, I . . .' but the rest of her words were lost as he took her into his arms crushing her against him.

'I agree,' murmured Richard huskily, 'now is the time for the perfect end to the evening.'

By the time Charmian realised what he was implying, he was carrying her upstairs kissing her at the same time. At last, she thought hazily, at last I'm going to be a whole woman. She wrapped her arms sublimely around his neck, and closing her eyes abandoned herself as she floated into a misty rapture. Her whole being ached with longing for him.

Richard laid her gently on the large bed, his hard body closing down mercilessly on hers. Then his mouth found hers again with renewed vigour. This kiss seemed to go on and on, dragging her into a vortex of sensuality that seemed to last for ever. She was aware of nothing but the sensations that were quivering through her body.

His hands found the back fastening of her dress and expertly undoing it, he peeled it down. She willingly helped by slipping her arms out of the long sleeves. He sank his face between her breasts, cupping them gently in his hands.

'Oh, you're so beautiful, so beautiful,' he groaned.

Charmian gasped with pleasure, arching her back to press herself even more closely to him. His mouth returned to her lips, tracing a tingling trail from her breast, pausing at the racing pulse in the delicate hollow of her throat. As his hard thighs pressed down on hers a shuddering wave of emotion welled within her.

All the time his hands were gently caressing her, stroking her, stimulating sensations she never knew existed. As she gasped again and instinctively arched her spine in response to the pressure of his hands, Richard gently slipped the rest of her dress down. The subdued lighting in the room added to the sensual intimacy as he finished undressing her slowly.

'Oh, Richard, Richard,' she whimpered, wanting to hear him say those precious words, *I love you.*

He gave a deep throaty chuckle as his teeth made a foray on her ear lobe.

'Oh, Charmian, Charmian,' he said huskily, 'Didn't I tell you that I always got what I wanted, and I want you.'

To Charmian those words were like an ice cold shower. *I always get what I want.* No words of endearment, just a flat statement of fact. He wanted her, he was going to take what he wanted.

Her hands that had been caressing started fighting and she pushed him away fiercely. All desire was gone in a flash. She was suddenly filled with disgust at herself, and filled with fear. Fear of being added to his conquests and then being forgotten for another woman when it suited him.

Suddenly his lovemaking seemed too expert. She fought to push him away more vigorously.

'Do you think I am going to stop now?' He uttered the words incredulously. 'I want you,' and his mouth came down powerfully on hers, almost crushing her into submission. But she fought back again and when he finally realised that she was in earnest, he suddenly let her go.

Trembling with anger he threw her roughly back on the bed and moved away.

He looked at her for a moment, his face black with fury then he turned away and furiously paced the room.

'Why, just tell me in God's name, why?' He spat the words at her.

'I wanted to. I wasn't pretending,' she said in a low voice, trembling with unshed tears.

'I thought I could. I thought . . .' she stopped. She couldn't say, *I thought you loved me*. She was too proud.

She fumbled desperately around the bed for her clothes, her face hot with shame. 'Suddenly my deep-rooted instincts surfaced,' she said. 'I know now that I shall only ever make love with a man that I love and who loves me. And as we don't love each other, I can't make love with you. Sorry,' she added in a small voice.

'You left it a little late to make up your mind,' snarled Richard. 'Nearly too bloody late.' His voice lashed at her like a whip.

Charmian sat on the edge of the bed, fully dressed by now, but her body still vibrated from the touch of his hands and lips. She felt desperately ashamed and couldn't bring herself to meet his eyes.

'I think I want to go home,' she said hollowly.

'I think perhaps you should. Not much point in staying here!' came the tight-lipped response.

Picking up his jacket he led the way downstairs, Charmian following miserably behind. The same stairs he had carried her up not so very long ago, when they had both been riding high on the crest of a wave of unthinking passion.

When they reached the kitchen door he stepped in front, Charmian thought to open the door, but he didn't. He barred her way with his arm and with his other hand he grasped the tip of her chin between his thumb and forefinger. Tilting her head back roughly, he forced her to look at him.

She had expected to see stormy anger in his eyes, but what she saw there puzzled her. She wasn't sure what he was thinking.

'Are you a virgin?' he demanded brusquely.

'Yes,' Charmian whispered simply in reply.

'I see,' was all he said. Then, abruptly letting go of her chin, he opened the door and led the way through the kitchen out to his car not speaking another word. It seemed the subject no longer interested him and neither, apparently, did she.

Charmian didn't know whether she was glad or sorry that he hadn't pursued the subject. She was almost regretting her inexperience. She wished she had been able to give him what he wanted, what she wanted too. But it was no use, she couldn't change her character.

Whatever his thoughts he gave no clue to them. Just silently drove her back to her flat. When they reached the house he opened the door for her politely, then drove swiftly away.

CHAPTER FOURTEEN

AFTER SHE had left Richard and let herself into her flat, Charmian didn't even try to go to bed. What was the point, she thought miserably. Nervously taut like a coiled spring, sleep was impossible. A multitude of conflicting emotions raced through her mind as she paced restlessly up and down the room.

She searched feverishly through the cupboards until she found a packet of cigarettes. Normally a non-smoker, the need to do something, anything, overwhelmed her.

Watching the blue smoke lazily twisting and curling in a wreath towards the ceiling somehow relaxed her and at last the tears came. Bathed in misery, the tears trickled slowly down her cheeks, leaving their bitter taste of salt on her lips.

She loved Richard as she had never loved any other man in her life, that she knew. There would never be another man. But he didn't love her. He found her attractive yes, and desirable, there was no doubt about that. But the most important thing was missing—love. He didn't love her. She knew that she could settle for nothing less than a lasting love, a commitment. That, she now acknowledged bitterly, was impossible. Total commitment wasn't in his scheme of things.

If he had felt anything for her at all, other than lust, he would have said so. But he had said nothing. After she had confessed to him that she was a virgin he had, to all intents and purposes, dismissed her contemptuously.

Her face burned, suffused with renewed heat from shame at the thought of him undressing her. What madness had made her behave so shamelessly?

By the time morning arrived Charmian knew what she must do. She must hand in her resignation and leave the unit and the friends she had made as soon as possible. To work with Richard after last night would be an impossibility.

Sitting down at her table in the kitchen, with a cup of coffee to try to steady her nerves, she penned the most difficult letter she had ever written. She asked if she could be excused her month's notice and gave the excuse of urgent personal reasons, asking that she should be released from her duties the following day. After sealing the letter she put on her uniform and went off for her last day's duty in the unit, delivering the note to the personnel office before she went on duty.

She also rang Sheila, a girlfriend in London, asking her if she could put her up for a few days. Sheila was delighted and even had enough spare room to store Charmian's trunks. So that was the immediate problem of where to go settled.

Once in the intensive care unit she made no mention of it to anyone, but tried to concentrate on her work. She saw Richard several times and her heart lurched unevenly at the sight of him, but apart from discussing various patients with her in a cold, businesslike manner, he ignored her. He spent most of the time closeted away in his office.

At about eleven that morning the internal telephone on Charmian's desk rang. It was Clarke Thomas. He had no idea of course of the real reason why Charmian had given in her notice, but had assumed it was some pressing family matter. Charmian let him think that. It was more convenient that way. He was very helpful and had made all the necessary arrangements so that Charmian could be released the next day.

Her duty dragged on endlessly—it seemed to go on for ever and ever, but at last the time came for Charmian to leave. Liz was not on duty that night, staff was, but Charmian knew Liz was due in the following morning and wrote her a brief note to explain her absence.

Her eyes were blurred with tears as she sealed the note in the envelope and left it propped up on the desk where she knew she would see it in the morning. There was so much she wanted to say, but just couldn't.

She walked slowly down the road leading from the hospital to her flat. The air was heavy with the scent from the lime trees that stood like silent sentinels in orderly lines each side of the road. She remembered her first walk down that same road in early spring. No leaves on the trees then, just the promise of things to come.

Now the house was wreathed in scarlet and pink climbing roses. A lone, late bee droned among them, searching out their nectar. Charmian stood silently drinking in their heady perfume. Closing her eyes she knew this memory would linger with her for ever. The scent of roses would always trigger off memories of this place and of Richard West.

She forced herself to pack everything that night, even though it was a daunting task. It was fortunate, she thought thankfully, that both John and Martin were on duty at other hospitals that night. That meant they wouldn't be down to ask any awkward questions.

Why couldn't I have fallen in love with someone like John, thought Charmian, miserably stuffing her belongings into her trunk. Someone so dependable and trustworthy.

It was two in the morning before Charmian finally finished packing. She left the clothes she needed out ready for the morning. She was by now utterly exhausted from her lack of sleep the night before and from the effort of packing, so she had no difficulty in falling asleep.

The morning sun streaming across her face through the open curtains of her bedroom awoke her. Glancing quickly at the clock she saw it was gone eight already. Damn, she had meant to get up earlier than that. Picking up the phone she dialled the railway to arrange for her trunk to be picked up and delivered to Sheila's flat in London. The pickup truck would come at eleven, she was informed. She would have preferred earlier, but that was the earliest time they could manage to arrange.

As she had plenty of time now, she made herself a coffee and put the rest of the contents of her cupboard on the top of the fridge. Then she wrote John a short note telling him that she was leaving to go back to London and promising to write to him soon. She also told him to take the food left inside the fridge and the stuff on the top.

That done she popped the note through John's front door and, returning to her own flat, she ran a bath and climbed in it. The phone rang. Charmian started to get out of the bath to answer, then suddenly realised it might be Liz or someone else from the unit. They must have read her note by now. Better she thought, that they think I've already left. So she let the phone ring and ring until it finally stopped. She was towelling herself dry when her front door bell rang.

Her heart thudded nervously. She didn't want to face anyone now. She wanted to leave without having to lie to anyone and she knew she couldn't possibly tell them the truth. It was too ridiculous. I can't say I've fallen in love with my boss, she thought grimly.

She waited, holding her breath. Perhaps if she kept very quiet they would go away thinking there was no one there.

But no, the bell rang again, longer and more persistently. Deciding reluctantly there was no alternative but to answer, Charmian slipped on her thin, blue cotton robe which luckily she hadn't packed and, tying the belt around her slim waist, opened the door.

Richard West swept in like a hurricane, waving a piece of paper which Charmian recognised as her letter to Liz in his hand.

'What is the meaning of this?' he demanded.

An agonising numbness constricted her throat. Unable to speak, Charmian backed away, nervously clutching her robe tightly around her.

Richard slammed the door violently shut behind him and advanced menacingly towards her, still waving the letter.

'I said what is the meaning of this?'

Charmian found her voice. 'It's not addressed to you,' she faltered.

'No. But it damn well should have been,' he retorted, 'and I want to know the reason. I have a right to know.'

'You have no right,' she whispered, unable to meet his eyes.

'Damn you, I have!' he thundered, his voice echoing round the room, the air vibrating with its resonance.

'I demand to know the reason,' he repeated.

Charmian could bear the agony no longer, he was making it so intolerably hard for her.

'All right,' she burst out, 'you want to know the reason, I'll tell you.' She turned away from him and abruptly crossed to the window, standing with her back to him so that he couldn't see her tear-brimmed eyes.

In a barely audible voice she said, 'It's because I've fallen in love with a man who doesn't love me. Because I've made a fool of myself and I can't go on working with him every day, because . . .' her voice broke in spite of herself. She could go on no longer.

'What is his name?' asked Richard's voice determinedly behind her.

Charmian winced. Did he have to be so cruel? Did he have to humiliate her? Couldn't he go, now that he knew the reason? But no, Richard persisted.

'What is his name?'

'It's you,' she whispered almost inaudibly, clenching her fists tightly until the knuckles gleamed white.

She felt Richard's hands on her shoulders. Gently but firmly he turned her towards him. Putting one hand under her chin he raised her trembling, tear-stained face to his.

'Say it again,' he commanded. 'Better still,' he added, 'say, *I love you, Richard*.'

Charmian searched his face wonderingly, thrown into strong relief as it was by the sunlight pouring in through the window. Strength and a fierce pride were etched in his face. But there was something else. That gentle tenderness she had glimpsed once before—only now she didn't just catch a glimpse of it, his whole face shone with it.

'I love you, Charmian,' he said gathering her into his arms.

'But I . . .' her words were lost as his lips sought hers, convincing her that his words rang true.

Much later, as Charmian struggled to try to assemble her confused slightly delirious senses, she whispered, to him. 'I still don't understand!' She ran her fingertips along the line of his strong jaw as if to reassure herself that he was real.

'I thought after the other night that you didn't want anything more to do with me and I can't say I blame you.'

Richard held her at arm's length, shaking his head and looking suddenly serious.

'I thought you didn't want anything to do with *me*,' he said, 'and I couldn't blame you! I've behaved like a headstrong fool since the first day I set eyes on you.' He brought her back into the tight fold of his arms and added, 'That was when I first fell in love with you.'

Again his lips sought hers, stirring familiar fires of passion. Then, showering her face and eyes with a million little kisses as light as butterfly wings, he carried her over to the settee and, sitting her in the corner, took a small box out of his pocket and gave it to her.

'Open it,' he said. 'I bought it the day after I met you because then I thought rashly that it wouldn't be long before I would be able to give it to you.'

He sat down beside her and put his arms around her.

'But that was before I found out you were involved with John Bourne, and then there was that wretched ballet dancer.'

'I wasn't involved, as you put it, with either of them,' protested Charmian.

'Maybe not,' he said, 'but you certainly gave me the cold shoulder.'

'But you were always with Carol,' accused Charmian, 'and then I thought . . . well I thought you just wanted to use me. Just to make love to me.'

'Well of course I did,' said Richard, gently stroking the back of her neck. 'And I still do want to make love to you,' he added, grasping a handful of her silvery hair and burying his face in it. 'But only on your terms, Charmian,' he said slowly. 'You were right the other night. Love is important. It's essential. Now, please, open the box.'

Slowly, with trembling fingers, Charmian opened the little box. Inside, a solitaire diamond ring shot flashes of ice blue and rose red fire at her from its shimmering depths. Taking the ring from its box Richard slipped it on the fourth finger of her left hand. Then taking her hand, he raised it to his lips and placed a warm and tender kiss in the palm. A thrill of pleasure ran through her. His dark eyes told her all she wanted to know.

'Will you marry me?' he asked quietly.

'Yes,' she said simply, sliding her arms around his neck.

She knew they had all the years ahead to talk about their love, there was no need for explanation now. The past was history, only the future was important.

'As soon as possible,' he whispered, 'I don't think I can wait very long.'

'As soon as possible,' she agreed, and reaching up she drew his dark head down to hers. 'I don't think I can wait very long either.'